MILLION-DOLLAR MYSTERY

Max handed the screwdriver to Stevie. He took the horse's nameplate and lined it up with the screw holes that were already in the stall door. Then he handed Stevie a screw and motioned for her to fasten the nameplate.

She stepped forward and read the new tenant's name for the first time.

"Honey-Pie?" she asked, astonished.

"That's right," said Max.

"That doesn't sound like a million-dollar horse," Carole protested. "That sounds like the kind of weird name an old lady would give her puppy!"

"Now you're getting warmer," said Max mysteriously, handing Stevie the second screw. He didn't say another word to the girls while Stevie finished fastening the nameplate to the door. He just smiled, took the screwdriver from Stevie, and walked back to his office, clearly enjoying every minute of his mystery.

"I'll be here on Monday," Lisa declared.

"I wouldn't miss it for . . . for—well, a million bucks," Stevie agreed.

"We'll *all* be here on Monday to welcome, um, Honey-Pie"—the sickly sweet name didn't come easily to Carole's lips—"to its . . . his . . . her new home."

the SADDLE CLUB

MILLION-DOLLAR HORSE

BONNIE BRYANT

A SKYLARK BOOK
NEW YORK • TORONTO • LONDON • SYDNEY • AUCKLAND

Special thanks to Laura Roper of Sir "B" Farms

RL 5, ages 009–012

MILLION-DOLLAR HORSE
A Bantam Skylark Book / May 2000

ISBN 0-553-48696-9

Visit us on the Web! www.randomhouse.com/kids
Educators and librarians, for a variety of teaching tools, visit us at
www.randomhouse.com/teachers

Published simultaneously in the United States and Canada

Bantam Skylark is an imprint of Random House Children's Books, a divi-
sion of Random House, Inc. SKYLARK BOOK and colophon and BAN-
TAM BOOKS and colophon are registered trademarks of Random House,
Inc. Bantam Books, 1540 Broadway, New York, New York 10036.

PRINTED IN THE UNITED STATES OF AMERICA
OPM   10 9 8 7 6 5 4 3 2 1

With many thanks, for many things,
this book is dedicated to Sandra Jordan.

"Look at this!" Stevie Lake said, pointing to a small picture in a large catalog. Her two best friends, Carole Hanson and Lisa Atwood, leaned over the page to see what had caught her interest.

"Isn't that the cutest?" Stevie's finger rested on a picture of a pink horse blanket with lace on the edge.

"Cute, but not practical," Carole said. "I mean, lace? In a stable? And pink? It would get dirty in an instant."

"I didn't mean I wanted to *buy* it," Stevie said. "I just meant it was cute."

"It is," Lisa agreed. "But I've never thought that pink was Belle's color. I've always thought she looked best in winter tones."

The three girls smiled, amused at the idea that a

1

horse had any fashion sense or color preferences. Stevie sighed and turned the page. There she found a wide selection of very sensible horse blankets in very sensible colors, like dark brown, dark green, dark blue, and gray.

"That's more like it," she said.

"And almost exactly as affordable," Carole said, noticing the prices.

"It doesn't cost anything to look," Stevie said, letting her eyes wander across the page to the beginning of the tack trunk section. "And besides, Belle doesn't even need a new blanket."

"Not needing something for our horses never kept us from window-shopping before," said Lisa.

"But this is different. In this case, not spending money may cost some horse its life," Carole reminded her friends somberly.

The three of them were sitting in the total comfort of the tack room at Pine Hollow Stables. It wasn't that the seats were all that comfortable. Lisa was perched on an overturned bucket, while Carole and Stevie lounged against stacked hay bales. It was that being in and around Pine Hollow was always comfortable for this threesome. It was their favorite place because it meant they were doing their favorite thing: anything to do with horses.

The three girls, so different in so many ways, had one gigantic thing in common: They were all horse-crazy. In fact, they were all so horse-crazy that they'd formed their own club, The Saddle Club. It had only two rules. The first was the easiest: All members had to be horse-crazy. The other wasn't so easy: It required them to help one another out whenever they needed it.

Often that meant Carole and Lisa had to help bail Stevie out of some trouble that her irrepressibly mischievous nature had lured her into. Stevie had an active imagination and a weird sense of humor. That pairing often got her in hot water. Fortunately, she was almost as clever at getting out of hot water as she was at getting into it. And that was where her friends came in—they always ended up helping her.

Lisa was the center of common sense in the group. She was a straight-A student who approached problems with cool logic—a useful counterbalance to Stevie's wild schemes and imagination. Stevie didn't have any of Lisa's organizational skills. For example, Stevie's idea of a nice outfit usually consisted of anything she *hadn't* had to pull out of the laundry pile, which often led to "interesting" color combinations with flying shirttails and clashing patterns. Lisa, however, always looked neat and tidy, perfectly matched and pressed. Their different approaches extended to other areas as well. While Stevie might begin a project and lose interest a third of the way into it, Lisa would pull through until the end.

Carole, on the other hand, might forget what the project was—unless it had to do with horses. When it came to her favorite subject, Carole never forgot anything. She might forget to comb her hair in the morning, but she'd never forget to comb her horse's mane or give him a grooming after a ride. She might forget to eat lunch, but she'd never forget to give Starlight his rations and fresh water.

Carole, whose mother had died of cancer a few years before, lived with her father, a colonel in the Marines, in a house on the edge of the town of Willow Creek, Virginia, where Pine Hollow Stables was. Stevie and Lisa both lived within walking distance of the stables. Lisa lived with her parents. She had an older brother, Peter, but he was living and studying in Europe, so she was almost an only child like Carole.

Stevie, on the other hand, frequently declared that she lived in a circus, and her friends enjoyed the relatively raucous atmosphere of the Lake household when they visited. Stevie had three brothers—one older, one younger, and one twin, and as the only girl, she often felt it fell to her to uphold the honor of womanhood. She did this by playing more practical jokes on her brothers than they played on her. It was a tough job, but somebody had to do it, and Stevie Lake was born for it. As a result, she spent a lot of time relinquishing her allowance to her parents or scraping gum off the undersides of desks at school, depending on where the punishment was delivered.

In spite of their differences, the common ground of horses drew Stevie, Lisa, and Carole together and kept them together. Saturday was almost invariably their favorite day, since they could devote almost the entire day to horses. It began with a Pony Club meeting, followed by a riding class. They usually followed that up with some stable chores and ended the day with a leisurely visit to the local ice cream parlor, where they usually talked about their favorite subject: horses.

The girls were devoted to horses, but they were also devoted to one another and would do anything to help one another out, so even the potentially onerous Rule Two of The Saddle Club was no problem for them, and they sometimes applied it to others. In other words, when someone else needed their help, they'd pitch in as a team. They thought of that as a Saddle Club project.

Sitting around in the tack room on that Saturday morning, they hatched just such a project.

"Judy Barker is the greatest, isn't she?" Lisa asked.

Stevie and Carole agreed. Judy was Pine Hollow's vet. She had just given a talk to Horse Wise, their Pony Club, as she often did. She'd discussed seasonal changes in feed, which the young riders all thought was very interesting; but they'd been even more interested in the other news Judy had for them.

Judy, who worked exclusively with horses, did volunteer work for CARL, the County Animal Rescue League, whenever CARL had a sick horse.

"I always prefer to treat a horse in its own home," Judy had told the group that morning. "They heal better in familiar surroundings, but sometimes the surroundings are the problem." The young riders knew what she meant. A horse might be abused and need to be taken away from its owner. Or an owner might have an inadequate home for a horse, for example, one that provided no shelter, and then the horse would have to be removed. Judy told the story of one owner who had died, leaving nothing behind but a horse and nobody to care for it.

"In all these cases, the horses had to be removed and taken to CARL. And every single time, CARL has had to borrow a trailer from someone. Well, it's time for CARL to have its own horse trailer. And we can do it—with your help.

"The Cross County Tack Shop has offered us a used trailer. It's a one-horse trailer, nothing special, but more than adequate for CARL's needs. The price is five hundred dollars, and they've promised that ten percent of everything our volunteers sell out of their catalog will go toward the purchase of the van. I've got a copy of the catalog for each of you. Now, you may not need anything—though I've never known a rider who didn't want to buy almost everything in the CC Tack Catalog—but if you do, go ahead and buy it from Cross County and get your friends, your neighbors, and even utter strangers to do the same, will you?"

They promised they would. This was a great deal for CARL and it wouldn't cost anybody a penny. All they had to do was find someone who wanted to spend five thousand dollars at the tack shop.

"Look, here's a saddle that would do the whole thing! Just one buyer and CARL will have its trailer!" Stevie said. She pointed to her latest catalog discovery.

"If you're a rhinestone cowboy," said Lisa.

"And if any self-respecting horse would wear the thing," Carole said.

Stevie had to agree. The saddle in question was a specialized item for dress rodeo wear—large, heavy, and showy, studded with sterling silver—hardly the kind of saddle Stevie and her English-riding friends would need. Besides, they all had perfectly good saddles—none of which cost anywhere near five thousand dollars.

"Here's something I want," Carole announced. "And I'm going to order it right this second."

Stevie looked over Carole's shoulder. "Great! I'm trying to find a buyer for a five-thousand-dollar saddle and Carole picks out a halter for four dollars."

"The longest journey begins with a single step," Lisa said philosophically.

"Sure," Stevie agreed. "I was just hoping the step might be bigger than the forty cents that'll earn toward CARL's trailer."

Carole tugged the order form out of the catalog and began filling in the blanks.

"Oh, it's you," a familiar voice greeted them.

Lisa was the only one who looked up, being too polite to ignore even the most unwelcome greeting.

"Yes, Veronica," she said. "Hello to you, too."

Veronica diAngelo was also a rider at Pine Hollow, a member of their Pony Club, and a classmate of Stevie's at Fenton Hall, a private school in Willow Creek. That was where Veronica's common ground with The Saddle Club stopped. She was the richest, snootiest girl any of them had ever had the burden of meeting. She considered herself way too good to hang around with the likes of The Saddle Club. She rode only purebred horses, and she talked only with purebred girls. She considered herself too good to do such common tasks as look after her own horse, clean her own tack, or help anyone else do anything. Her usual way of caring for her Thoroughbred, Danny, was to complain about the way Red, Pine Hollow's head stable hand, did *her* work.

The Saddle Club didn't have much time for Veronica and generally tried to avoid her. But if there was one thing of which Veronica seemed to have an endless supply, it was money.

"We're just looking through the Cross County catalog," Lisa said. "Have you seen all the neat things they have? Isn't it great that if we buy things from them we can help earn the money for CARL's new trailer?"

"Oh," said Veronica, as if she hadn't been there for Judy's presentation.

"You're going to buy something, aren't you?" Lisa persisted.

"From Cross County?" Veronica asked, wrinkling her nose as if she smelled something bad. Lisa was undeterred.

"Stevie saw a really nice saddle. . . ."

"As you already know, I have all my saddles made for me," Veronica said.

"Oh, right, but how about other things, like a blanket, or . . . I noticed a scratch on Danny's tack trunk—"

"I'm having that refinished," Veronica told her. "And Danny's new blanket is coming from Scotland this week."

"But what about CARL?" Lisa asked. "Don't you want to help?"

"Why should I?" Veronica asked with a genuinely puzzled look on her face. "I mean, those horses are really just worthless animals, aren't they? I don't understand what all the fuss is about."

Not for the first time, The Saddle Club was struck dumb by the depth of Veronica's insensitivity. None of them could think of a thing to say while Veronica finished selecting a lead rope from the overhead rack and then left.

They were still sitting in stunned silence when Max Regnery, the owner of Pine Hollow, came into the tack room.

"Oh, good, I'm so glad you're still here. I've got a little job for you," he said.

"I knew we should have left for TD's already," Stevie said. TD's was the ice cream shop.

"Oh, this won't take long," Max said, a twinkle in his eye.

"Oops," said Carole, thinking Stevie was right. Max's idea of a little chore sometimes took up a whole afternoon. Still, although the girls might complain about it, they knew that the work they did around the stable was important. It was important for the horses, but it was important for them as well. All the riders were expected to pitch in, and that was one of the most important ways Pine Hollow kept its costs down.

"Okay, so where's the moving van full of hay we have to unload?" Carole teased.

"Or the fifty-foot manure pile we have to move?" Stevie asked.

"Or the trunk full of tack that we should be able to see our faces in by the time we leave?" Lisa added.

"Follow me," Max said. "Oh, and bring along some pitchforks and a wheelbarrow."

"So what else is new?" Stevie said, stuffing the Cross County catalog into her back pocket.

"I THOUGHT WE already mucked out all the stalls," Stevie protested while she pushed the wheelbarrow down the aisle after Max.

"You did," he said.

"And?"

"Right this way, ladies," Max said, turning one corner of the U-shaped stable. He stopped at the large corner box stall.

"The foaling stall?" Carole said. "Are we going to have a new baby in the house?"

"Nope," Max said. He unlatched the gate for them and they entered the extra-large box stall.

Although Pine Hollow was primarily for riders, both owners and renters, Max had expanded into breeding a while back when he'd acquired a valuable stallion named Geronimo. It was the usual practice to have mares who were about to foal come to the stable to have their little ones. Soon after the birth, they could be bred again, so it made sense to have them near the stallion at that time. The girls had enjoyed helping out with more than one foaling. Apparently, though, this wasn't why they were cleaning the stall.

The stall wasn't really dirty. It had been cleaned out after the last resident had left a few months earlier. But if a new horse was going to live there, the stall needed a good sweeping and some fresh shavings.

"So, tell us about the new visitor," Carole said, now very curious.

"Resident," Max corrected her. "This horse is arriving Monday afternoon and will be living here permanently."

"In the foaling stall?" Lisa asked.

"For now," Max said. "Eventually, we may build an extension."

"An extension for just one animal? This must be a valuable horse," Stevie said.

"In a way," Max said. "A very real way. In fact, I guess you'd say it was a million-dollar horse."

"A million bucks?" Stevie said, her jaw dropping.

"A million dollars?" Veronica echoed. She'd just

13

been passing by, but the words *million* and *dollars* in one sentence would always be enough to catch her attention.

"Yes, a million dollars," Max said to her pointedly.

"Well, I suppose a horse like my Danny would fetch almost that much—if I were of a mind to sell him, which, of course, I'm not."

Everybody there knew perfectly well that, valuable as Danny was, he was not worth anywhere near a million dollars.

"Well, Veronica, if your horse is so valuable, perhaps you could explain to me why it is that Red tells me you left his stall door unlatched *again* . . . ," said Max.

"He claimed I did it?" she asked.

"Well, since Danny's your horse, it's your responsibility to latch the door when you put him away after a ride."

"I'm not at all sure that Red wasn't the one who put him in his stall."

"I'm sure you tried to get him to do it . . . ," Max said, allowing the implications to hang in the air.

"You'll have to speak to Red about that," Veronica said.

"I have," said Max. "I take my responsibility to our resident horses seriously. I can't be responsible for the owners, however. See that it doesn't happen again."

14

"Well, then, *I'll* speak to Red," said Veronica as she moved on down the hallway, indicating that the conversation was over.

Stevie, Lisa, and Carole all looked at one another, stifling giggles. It was always a glorious moment to see Veronica (a) caught doing something unforgivable like leaving a stall unlatched, and (b) getting bawled out for it. They didn't want to let Max see their glee, however. Veronica's oversight was foolish and dangerous to her horse. Max didn't take anything that imperiled a horse lightly, and neither did they.

"Million-dollar snob," Stevie whispered to her friends.

"Ahem," Max said, letting them know he'd overheard. It was enough to remind them that they had a job to do, and a weird one at that. Since it wasn't a mare about to foal that was going to live in the foaling stall, what was it?

"I bet it's another stallion," Carole said.

"Why do you say that?" Max asked.

"Well, because stallions can be sort of temperamental and need space. Also, this has a small paddock attached, and that would allow the stallion to be outdoors but kept separate from the other horses. Am I right?"

"Your logic is good, but your conclusion is wrong. It's not a stallion."

Stevie heaved a load of shavings on the floor, and while Lisa and Carole smoothed it out with pitchforks, she shared her idea.

"It's a show horse and it's in training," she declared.

"Nope," said Max.

Lisa had an idea. "It's not in training, it's already been trained and it's won a zillion ribbons. The horse needs the extra wall space for the cabinets that contain its trophies."

"Nope," said Max.

For a moment Carole leaned on her pitchfork. "The most valuable horses around here are the best of the schooling horses. If a stable like Pine Hollow has a new and great schooling horse, one that any student can ride at any level, that's like a treasure. I bet that's what's coming."

"Nope," said Max.

He was definitely not being helpful.

"Come on, Max. Tell us," said Stevie, brimming with curiosity.

"Well, I'll tell you one thing," he said.

"Yes?" Lisa asked.

"You're not even close." He grinned mischievously. Stevie tossed a handful of shavings at him.

"And flattery will get you nowhere. Hard work might, however."

With that, he left the three of them to complete the

chore. It wasn't hard to do and it was certainly something they'd done often enough to be able to finish without supervision.

"This is strange," said Stevie, ever interested in a mystery.

"It's probably that Max doesn't have a permanent stall available right now and that's why he's using the foaling stall," said Lisa.

It was logical, but it didn't fit in with Max's contention that this was a million-dollar horse and that he might eventually build an extension on the stable for it.

"Maybe it's a really rare breed or something," said Carole, trying to think what kind of horse would be so unusual that it would be worth a million dollars.

"Maybe it's just really big, like a Clydesdale, and it's too big for a regular stall," said Lisa.

"They can be valuable, but usually in matched sets, like the ones that pull that beer wagon," said Carole. "And a million dollars? No way. Not even the ones that pull the beer wagon."

They were stumped, but speculating made the time pass quickly as they finished the work on the stall. Just as Carole was smoothing out the last scoopful of wood shavings, Max returned. He was carrying something in one hand and a screwdriver in the other.

"Ah, the name!" Carole said. "Maybe it's like *Secretariat!*"

"Secretariat's dead," Lisa reminded her. The Triple Crown–winning stallion had been worth a million dollars at least. "And besides, Max said it wasn't a stallion."

Max handed the screwdriver to Stevie. He took the horse's nameplate and lined it up with the screw holes that were already in the stall door. Then he handed Stevie a screw and motioned for her to fasten the nameplate.

She stepped forward and read the new tenant's name for the first time.

"Honey-Pie?" she asked, astonished.

"That's right," said Max.

"That doesn't sound like a million-dollar horse," Carole protested. "That sounds like the kind of weird name an old lady would give her puppy!"

"Now you're getting warmer," Max said mysteriously, handing Stevie the second screw. He didn't say another word to the girls while Stevie finished fastening the nameplate to the door. He just smiled, took the screwdriver from Stevie, and walked back to his office, clearly enjoying every minute of his mystery.

"I'll be here on Monday," Lisa declared.

"I wouldn't miss it for . . . for—well, a million bucks," Stevie agreed.

"I bet whatever kind of horse it is—and I'm pretty sure Honey-Pie *is* a horse—is going to take a lot of extra care," said Carole. "That's got to be why Max wanted us to help out in the first place, and I know he'll need us to help out in the future. We'll *all* be here on Monday to welcome, um, Honey-Pie"—the sickly sweet name didn't come easily to her lips—"to its . . . his . . . her new home."

"Sure we will," Stevie agreed. She picked up the handles to the wheelbarrow and began to push it back to where it was stored next to the tack room. Her friends carried the pitchforks. They'd finished preparing Honey-Pie's new home, and now it was time to head for TD's.

They stowed their gear, washed up, and changed into street clothes. They'd long since discovered that they were not always welcome in public places if they smelled as if they'd just been doing a lot of hard and heavy work in a barn.

A few minutes later, they settled into their favorite booth and gave the waitress their order. As usual, Carole and Lisa ordered items most people would consider normal. Lisa wanted a dish of caramel frozen yogurt. Carole asked for a small hot fudge sundae with vanilla ice cream. Stevie was also true to her usual form.

"I'd like mint chocolate chip ice cream with pineapple chunks and, um, butterscotch sauce," she said.

The waitress winced.

"And, please, may I have some rainbow sprinkles?"

"Whipped cream?"

"Of course, but no cherry. I think the flavor would clash with the pineapple," Stevie said.

"We wouldn't want that, now, would we?" the waitress asked, fleeing before Stevie could add anything else to her concoction.

Carole brought out the Cross County catalog and resumed the job of filling out the order form for Starlight's new halter.

"There must be something else you want," Lisa said, still saddened by the fact that among the three of them their order would bring in only forty cents for CARL.

"There isn't anything else that I want or that Starlight needs," Carole said. "But I can think of a few people who might be interested in all sorts of goodies."

"Like?" Stevie asked.

"Well, for one thing, you can call Phil," Carole said. "I know he shops at Cross County all the time. He can certainly buy something from the catalog."

"And I bet A.J. needs something, too," Stevie said enthusiastically. "Okay, so if they each buy a halter, too, that'll make it a dollar twenty for CARL." Phil was Stevie's boyfriend, and A.J. was his best friend. They both lived in a nearby town and rode horses at Cross County Stables.

"And then I'm going to call Kate and her parents," said Carole.

"Wow," said Lisa, impressed with Carole's idea. Kate Devine's parents owned a dude ranch out West that the girls had visited many times. A place like the Bar None needed all sorts of equipment all the time. "If all they needed were a few saddles, well, that would really mount up quickly—pun not intended," she said.

"Even if they don't buy any silver-studded ones," said Stevie.

"And the next thing you know, the horses CARL rescues will be riding in style," said Carole.

"Just like they're worth a million bucks," said Lisa.

3

WHEN STEVIE ARRIVED at Pine Hollow on Monday, she found her two friends perched on the top rail of the fence that enclosed the stable's schooling ring. They were facing the driveway, obviously still awaiting the arrival of Honey-Pie.

"No sign of her yet?" Stevie asked.

"Max said she's supposed to be here by four," said Lisa.

"It's after that now," Carole observed, looking at her watch.

"It probably took extra time to pack all her jewelry," joked Stevie.

Lisa laughed, but Carole just looked tired. It wasn't easy for Carole to joke about horses, and everybody knew that horses didn't need jewelry to look beautiful.

A good grooming would do that just fine, as far as Carole was concerned.

Stevie was glad to have a few minutes with her friends before Honey-Pie's arrival. She had some news.

"Phil ordered a saddle blanket and A.J. said he was going to talk to his parents about getting a new tack trunk," she announced proudly.

"That's great!" said Lisa, mentally toting up the money going to CARL. "And if you add in the gloves my parents said I could buy, that'll come to almost fifteen dollars toward the trailer."

Carole had news of her own on that front. "The Devines asked me to send them the whole catalog," she said. "Frank said he didn't know for sure that the dude ranch needed anything, but he was going to check and promised he'd place any orders through us for CARL."

Stevie was so pleased to hear that, she clapped Carole on the back, which resulted in Carole's losing her balance and almost falling into the ring.

"I don't think they have back braces in the catalog," Lisa said, steadying Carole.

"Sorry about that," Stevie said. "I just got a little excited."

"It's okay," Carole said good-naturedly, settling herself back onto the rail. "It's for a good cause."

While Lisa and Stevie were asking Carole if she was

really all right and Carole was assuring them that she was, they nearly missed the arrival of a horse van in the yard.

The van, from a commercial leasing operation, was followed by two cars, a silver Volvo and a black Jaguar, all of which gave the impression of a parade, and that seemed fitting for a million-dollar horse.

The van came to a stop and the cars parked nearby. While the driver of the van stayed in the cab, filling out papers, the drivers of the other two cars eagerly approached the back of the van.

Neither one of them was dressed to be anywhere near a stable. The driver of the Volvo was older than the other, with gray hair and a tidy mustache. He was wearing a double-breasted pinstripe suit, a white shirt, and a striped tie.

"A lawyer," Stevie declared.

"How do you know?" Lisa whispered.

"Both my parents are lawyers," Stevie reminded her. "I can smell them from a thousand miles away. Besides, look at his shoes."

Lisa and Carole obeyed. "What about his shoes other than that they don't belong in a stable?" Carole asked.

"Wing tips," Stevie said. "It's a dead giveaway."

Carole and Lisa weren't as tuned in to the clothing preferences of the legal profession as Stevie was, but they had to agree that the overall look of the older man was definitely staid and, well, lawyerly.

"Okay, so what about the other guy?" Carole asked.

"I don't know, but he's not a lawyer," Stevie said.

"Definitely not a lawyer," Carole agreed. "He looks more like someone on vacation than a working lawyer."

"Permanent vacation," Lisa said. "I mean, I spend enough time shopping with my clothes-conscious mother to know that he's wearing very expensive casual clothes. The shoes are Gucci, the slacks Armani, and the sweater—well, I'm not sure who made it, but it's got to be pure cashmere. And I'll bet you his socks are, too."

"That's all expensive stuff, right?" Carole asked.

"Let me put it this way," Lisa said. "We could swap him for a horse trailer for CARL and have change left over."

Carole shook her head. "What a waste of money," she said.

"Not if you've got a lot more of it," Lisa said. "Someone who drives a Jaguar and dresses like that is bound to be a millionaire."

"But a dumb one," said Stevie. "I mean, it's dumb to wear expensive clothes like that to handle a horse."

"Not that he's actually handling the horse," said Carole, who had not taken her eyes from the goings-on. Usually with a newcomer, the girls hurried to welcome the horse and help the owners, but Max had been so mysterious about Honey-Pie that they were reluctant to butt in. The men, who they presumed were the horse's owners, were proceeding on their own. If they wanted help, they could ask for it.

The two had gone around to the rear of the van. "I've got it," said the older man.

"No, I can do it, Ben," said the other.

"I'm going to do this myself, Paul," said the lawyer apparently named Ben. "I have to protect this horse."

"Like I don't care?" Paul asked.

"Hmmph," said Ben.

Ben reached for the van's door handles and held them with his fingertips, trying to unlatch the door without getting any mud on his suit—which, as Lisa pointed out, could also be swapped for a trailer for CARL. "A thousand dollars at least," she muttered to her friends.

But the younger man, Paul, was taller and had longer arms. Eventually he managed to undo the latch. They swung the doors wide open. Inside the four-horse van was a lone mare, a honey-colored chestnut.

Together, because it was clear that neither of them could have managed it alone, they pulled out a ramp. Paul walked up the ramp gingerly, leaving Ben down at the end of it.

And then the girls saw something they'd never seen

before—a level of such total incompetence and igno-
rance about horses that they were stunned into silence.

Paul unlatched the gate on the stall where Honey-Pie
had been secured while traveling and stood back, pre-
sumably to let her wander down the ramp on her own.

Ben, standing at the base of the ramp, uttered the im-
mortal words, "Here, boy! Here, boy!" and clapped his
hands.

Any fool could have told him Honey-Pie was a mare.

The Saddle Club knew a disaster in the making
when they saw one. Without any discussion, the three of
them hopped off the fence and hurried over to the van.

Carole climbed into the van, located a lead rope,
clipped it to the mare's halter, and brought her down the
ramp, easy as could be. As soon as Carole and the mare
reached the ground, Stevie fished in her pocket and
found a piece of carrot (she almost always had a horse
treat in one pocket or another) and rewarded the horse
for her good behavior.

Lisa reached up and gave Honey-Pie a warm welcom-
ing pat and then a hug. The horse's sweet nature was so
evident by the way she'd obediently come down the ramp
that the girls all knew exactly why somebody had named
this lovely horse Honey-Pie. That was what she was.

"What a great horse!" Carole said, admiring her

strong lines and the eager and alert way her ears perked, listening for interesting sounds around her.

"She's wonderful!" Stevie said, rubbing the soft graying nose and looking deep into the mare's wise old eyes.

"She's really old," said Paul.

Carole took a look in her mouth. "Not that old," she said. "Maybe fifteen. This horse has a lot of good years left in her, and you don't have to worry. She'll get the best care in the world here at Pine Hollow."

"I'm sure," Paul said unenthusiastically.

"I'd like to have a discussion with Mr. Regnery about that," said Ben. "Is he around or does he entrust all his horses to little girls?"

"He's around," Stevie said, a little put off. "He's in the office, which is through that door and to your right. We can take Honey-Pie to her new home while you talk with Ma—uh, Mr. Regnery." Nobody Stevie knew had ever called Max that before, but if this was a million-dollar horse, then Max was a million-dollar stable owner, and if that meant calling him Mr. Regnery sometimes, well, she could do that.

The two men picked their way through the soft mud of the stable yard toward the door while the girls led the mare across the turf to the double door of the stable.

They could hardly wait until they were out of hearing distance of the two owners.

" 'Here, *boy*'?" Lisa said. That was enough to make the three of them dissolve into giggles. The idea that a horse could be called like a dog and that the owner didn't know the sex of his horse was too weird.

"I've got it," Stevie said. "They're from another planet!"

"Does that mean this is an alien horse?" Lisa asked.

"No, this is a very earthly horse," Carole assured her. "I mean, look at this sweetie. Did you ever see a nicer horse?"

They didn't think they had. They'd seen horses with better conformation, they'd seen horses that were more valuable in the sense of being purebreds, and they'd seen horses that had more striking coloring than Honey-Pie's pale chestnut coat, but they didn't think they'd ever seen a horse that had so immediately struck them as just plain nice.

The horse followed them obediently into her new stall. She looked around at the large foaling box, sniffed, shifted her ears, nuzzled the fresh shavings, and then sampled the hay in the tick. Once she was satisfied with that, she took a sip from the water bucket and looked directly at the three girls, as if to thank them.

"You're welcome," Carole said, producing another bit of carrot, which Honey-Pie took politely.

Stevie patted Honey-Pie's cheek and declared that

she'd be happy to pay a million bucks for a sweet horse like this—if she had the million. But she was only joking. Honey-Pie was sweet, all right, but this was not a million dollars' worth of horse. Not by a long shot. Honey-Pie was clearly mixed-breed—and so thoroughly mixed that none of the girls could identify any particular bloodline. She was probably beyond the age at which she could be bred, so she couldn't be considered valuable in that way. She'd do fine as a schooling horse, if that was why she was there, but nobody would pay that kind of money for a schooling horse. She was too old for any serious competition, showing, endurance, or racing.

In short, there was nothing about her that was worth a million dollars, except, it seemed, her personality.

The girls could hear Max approaching with Honey-Pie's two owners.

"Of course," he said. "All our horses get the best care."

"No expense should be spared," Ben said.

"None ever is," said Max. "All our horses receive first-rate care."

"Top-drawer," said Paul.

"That too," Max said.

The girls exchanged glances. Nobody who knew Max would ever think he'd slight any horse in his charge.

"And we only want your best stable hands looking after Honey-Pie when you can't give her your personal attention."

"I have only the best stable hands," Max said. "And now I can introduce you to three of them." He stopped at Honey-Pie's stall and indicated The Saddle Club.

"This is your idea of top drawer?" Ben asked.

"I'd like you to meet Carole, Stevie, and Lisa. All the riders here have learned proper care of horses, and they all pitch in to help look after our horses."

"But what do these little girls know?" Ben asked.

"We know how to unload a horse from a van," Stevie said as politely as she could manage.

"And girls, I'd like you to meet Mr. Benjamin Stookey," Max said, indicating the lawyer, "and Mr. Paul Fredericks."

"How do you do?" Lisa asked. The men nodded at all three girls but didn't acknowledge them much beyond that.

"Look, you're already paying me extra to house Honey-Pie in this large stall, and I'm sure that's all the extra consideration she needs. She'll have access to the little paddock . . ."

Recognizing a cue when she heard one, Lisa opened the double door at the back of the stall to show the men the little paddock.

". . . and from time to time, we'll let her out into

the pasture. Of course, the best thing of all would be to have her ridden occasionally."

"No way!" said Mr. Stookey.

"But it's good for saddle horses," Carole protested.

"And they like it," Stevie added.

"And I just bet this girl loves to be ridden," Lisa said, stroking the horse's neck.

"Honey-Pie is retired," Mr. Stookey said, making his declaration with finality. "She's not to be ridden."

"By anyone," Mr. Fredericks added.

"As you wish," said Max.

Carole scowled at him, but the look he gave her indicated that this was neither the time nor the place to argue.

"But we will give her pasture time," said Max.

"Is that wise?" Mr. Stookey asked.

The girls had never heard anybody question Max's judgment before. What surprised them more than that, however, was the fact that Max just let them go ahead and do it.

"I'm sure it is," said Max. "A horse's natural habitat is in fields and pastures. The worst thing you can do to a healthy young horse like Honey-Pie is to keep her cooped up in a stall and a tiny paddock. She really ought to be ridden several times a week."

"No riding. And what about the weather?" Mr. Fredericks asked.

"We don't put the horses out in bad weather, sir," Max said. "And when there's a chill in the air, they all have blankets on them."

"Good ones?"

"Not cashmere," Max said pointedly. "But warm ones."

"Ben," said Paul, as if to protest leaving Honey-Pie with Max.

"This place comes highly recommended," Mr. Stookey said to the younger man.

"Well, for now, then, I guess," Mr. Fredericks assented with a shrug.

"Well, since Honey-Pie seems to have settled in and these girls are seeing to her needs, why don't we go back to my office and finish up the paperwork so that you two can be on your way?"

Without further ado, the three men headed back toward the office.

"I never saw anything like that!" said Stevie once the office door had closed.

"Imagine! Questioning Max's judgment!" Lisa said.

"That's bad enough, but then saying this sweet thing can't be ridden!" Carole added.

"Well, she may be a million-dollar horse," Stevie said, "but I think she's owned by two twenty-five-cent idiots."

"Eloquent," Lisa said. Carole agreed.

4

"YOU WON'T BELIEVE what I just saw in Max's office!" Veronica diAngelo said breathlessly to Lisa, Stevie, and Carole, who were still standing by Honey-Pie's new stall.

"Two idiots who don't know anything about either horses or Max Regnery?" Stevie suggested.

"I don't know about that," Veronica said dismissively. "But it was definitely two men who know how to dress!"

The Saddle Club exchanged glances. It was completely typical of Veronica to notice clothes and pay no attention to the sweet old mare in the stall next to where she was standing.

"Not exactly barn wear," Lisa said.

"Nothing to wear while delivering a million-dollar horse," Stevie said.

That was when Veronica noticed Honey-Pie. Her eyes traveled over the horse as quickly and as disdainfully as they would over a woman wearing an off-the-rack dress.

"What million-dollar horse?" she asked, looking around for something more obviously valuable.

"This one." Carole gestured toward Honey-Pie.

Veronica's brows furrowed. "Oh, no," she said. "There's some mistake. This horse isn't worth . . ." They could see the calculator in her brain working. Finally Veronica shrugged. "She wouldn't fetch five hundred dollars from a glue factory," she said.

"Neither would you," said Stevie.

Veronica had started to go off in a huff when Max came out of his office with Mr. Stookey and Mr. Fredericks. Because Honey-Pie's stall was near the barn's exit, Veronica stopped short, getting another look at the elegant clothing the two men wore as they walked toward the front of the barn.

She was still admiring the cut of Mr. Stookey's suit when Max came over to talk to the girls.

"Max, I think there's been a terrible mistake, as you can surely see," said Veronica. "They've brought the wrong horse. It must have been the van driver's fault.

35

You know how careless they can be, and I guess the men never looked. . . ."

"Veronica, I'd like you to meet Honey-Pie, our newest resident," Max said, pointing to the old mare. "And there is no mistake."

"Piff," she said, dismissing the horse altogether. "I guess I'm the only one here who knows anything about valuable horses," she muttered. "So I'll go look after my own Thoroughbred." She turned on her heel and headed down the stable aisle.

"Maybe I should give her directions to Danny's stall," Stevie suggested. "I think that's the first time I've ever known her to go there to look after her horse."

"That's enough, Stevie," Max said, but Stevie would have sworn that there was a little smile on his lips. "I've got a lot more paperwork to fill out for our new guest, so I hope you'll continue to make her feel welcome and show her around a little bit."

"Count on us, Max," Carole said.

"I always do."

The girls went back into the oversized box stall and gave Honey-Pie a quick grooming. She clearly loved every minute of it, especially the part where Carole gave her another bit of carrot at the end as a reward for standing still.

Lisa reopened the door to the little paddock then,

and the bright light drew Honey-Pie's attention. Carole went to snap the lead line back on her halter, but Honey-Pie nudged her away and headed for the door on her own.

Stevie laughed. "I guess she doesn't need any help from us to find her way outside!"

"I guess not," Carole agreed, tucking the lead rope into her back pocket.

The girls followed Honey-Pie into the paddock. It wasn't a large space, but it had a pretty view of the Virginia countryside and the hills that surrounded Pine Hollow. Honey-Pie looked longingly at the fields and the woods beyond.

"She'd love a good trail ride, wouldn't she?" Lisa asked.

"You heard the orders," said Carole. "This old girl isn't going to go any farther than the large paddock on the other side of the barn."

"If that's retirement, I don't want any," said Stevie.

"I agree, and so must Honey-Pie," said Carole, observing the horse. "But owners are owners, and until Max convinces them otherwise, they have the last word on their horse's treatment."

"If only they had a clue," said Lisa. "I sure wonder who those guys are and how they came to own Honey-Pie. I never saw more reluctant—"

"—or more ignorant—" Carole said.

"—that too—owners in my life," Lisa completed her thought.

"It's a mystery," said Stevie, looking intrigued at the very word.

"Well, the good news is that Honey-Pie is out of their incompetent hands and into our competent ones!" Carole said. "And my experience tells me she's ready to have some time to herself."

Lisa and Stevie agreed. They left the mare in her little paddock, with the door open so that she could come back into her stall whenever she wanted. Everything that needed to be done had been done for Honey-Pie.

The girls changed into their street clothes and were going to stop by Max's office to say good-bye when they noticed that the black Jaguar was back in the driveway and heard Mr. Fredericks's voice coming from inside Max's office. The door was open and it was hard not to overhear the conversation.

"It just seems to me that they know what they're doing," Mr. Fredericks was saying.

"They do. And so do other people here, Mr. Fredericks."

"Call me Paul."

"Sure, Paul," said Max.

"Those little girls are what Honey-Pie needs," said Mr. Fredericks.

Stevie, Lisa, and Carole stopped in the hallway where neither Max nor Mr. Fredericks could see them. Mr. Fredericks was talking about them. He seemed to be urging Max to let them act as Honey-Pie's exclusive caretakers.

"We could pay extra," Mr. Fredericks said. "I mean, if the girls would like it."

"You don't have to pay extra, Mr.—"

"Paul."

"Right, uh, Paul. Every horse gets the best of care and the care is given by whomever I say, whenever I say. I cannot let you tell me who is going to look after Honey-Pie."

"But they seem so good!"

The girls beamed at the compliment from Mr. Fredericks.

"I decide these things," said Max. "Every young rider needs experience in horse care, and when each of them is ready, he or she is allowed to take on responsibilities. But not until I say so."

That stung. It sounded to Carole as if Max didn't think they had the necessary skills to look after Honey-Pie. Didn't he trust them? He'd just told Mr. Stookey they knew what they were doing. Why was he now telling Paul they didn't? What had they done wrong?

They wanted to hear more of the conversation, but it was interrupted.

Veronica diAngelo, apparently unaware that she had brushed past Stevie, Lisa, and Carole in the hallway, and oblivious to the fact that Max was having a serious discussion with Paul Fredericks, stormed into the office unannounced—her usual manner of arrival.

"That Red!" she huffed. "You won't believe what he did, or rather what he didn't do!" She was well into her spiel before she even noticed Paul Fredericks, in spite of his expensive clothes. "It's so typical of him, Max! You must do something about him. He doesn't know the first thing about looking after a *really* valuable horse!"

"Veronica!" Max said, trying to halt her tirade.

"Don't you 'Veronica' me!" she answered through her teeth. "I won't be put off this time! He's placed my horse in danger!"

"Veronica, you are interrupting me," Max said. "Excuse me, Mr. Fredericks, but this is Veronica diAngelo, and she doesn't always notice when someone is in the middle of a conversation."

"Oh, hello," said Veronica, and then, without missing a beat, continued with her diatribe about Red O'Malley, Pine Hollow's head stable hand, whom Veronica some-

40

times viewed as her personal servant. "He is extremely lax in the care of the stable's most valuable horse, my Danny. Need I remind you how many blue ribbons my horse has won? Or how much my father pays you to give him the best of care?"

"Veronica, we'll talk later," Max said, cutting her off completely. He turned to Mr. Fredericks. "I am sorry about this interruption, but I just want to assure you that you have not made a mistake by leaving Honey-Pie in our care."

Mr. Fredericks smiled warmly. "I'm sure you're right," he said, shaking Max's offered hand. "I know now that I can trust you and your staff to give Honey-Pie exactly the kind of care and attention she deserves." He exited Max's office and was in his Jaguar before Max completely exploded at Veronica.

Carole, Lisa, and Stevie had heard it all before and didn't want to be around while Max was furious at anyone. So, as Max explained very clearly that it was extremely rude to interrupt when he was having a conversation with someone else and while he told Veronica that if she looked after her own horse the way every single other owner did, perhaps she'd be more pleased with the care he got, The Saddle Club left Pine Hollow for the day.

They had some things to think about and some things

to talk about. Veronica's being angry and petulant was not news, but Max's remarks to Mr. Fredericks about how his students took on responsibilities only when he said so were very curious. It was true, of course, but the implication was that The Saddle Club wasn't necessarily ready to take on the responsibility of looking after Honey-Pie. What had they done to make Max lose confidence in them so suddenly?

"I DON'T UNDERSTAND," Lisa said. "I thought we were
doing everything just right for Honey-Pie."

"Honey-Pie seemed to think so, too," said Stevie, recalling the sweet way the horse had behaved.

"Well, except for the part about wanting to put a lead
on her to take her out to the paddock," Carole said,
smiling at the memory.

"Wasn't that cute?" Lisa asked, thinking of the
surprised look on Carole's face when the horse nudged
her.

"Honey-Pie has got to be the easiest horse I've ever
looked after," said Stevie. "Maybe when Max said she
was a million-dollar horse, he meant that was how much
the owners saved in trouble. Some horses . . ."

43

She didn't have to explain. Her friends knew that many horses had quirks that made them hard to look after. One wanted to be led only from the right-hand side; another would eat only feed without corn in it. Some horses wouldn't go into a paddock; some seemed at ease only with men or only with women. Prancer, the horse Lisa rode most of the time, was much more comfortable with young riders than with adults. Honey-Pie, on the other hand, seemed to be completely quirkless, unless you counted the fact that she could walk out into the paddock without any help from Carole!

"We can give her the best care," Lisa said.

"I know it, you know it, and I thought Max knew it," Stevie said. "So why did he tell Mr. Call-me-Paul different?"

"Beats me," said Lisa.

"It's a mystery," said Stevie. "You know, that's the second time I've said that in the last hour or so about Honey-Pie."

"I noticed," Lisa said.

"There's a lot about that horse that's mysterious," Carole confirmed.

"I'm beginning to think we're going to have to do some sleuthing," Stevie said.

"Don't be silly," Lisa said. "The most important thing

we can do for that horse is look after her. If Max doesn't think we know what we're doing, we're going to have to work extra hard, for her and for ourselves. We have to save our reputations."

"I can't disagree," Stevie said. "Still, I'd like to know what's going on. Really."

"Oh, we'll learn, all in good time," said Carole. "For now, it's just going to be fun to take care of Honey-Pie."

The three girls had arrived at the shopping center. It was just a small strip mall, but it had two attractions that made it extremely important to them. The first was TD's and the second was the bus stop. Stevie and Lisa each lived a few short blocks from Pine Hollow, and only a few houses from one another, but Carole's house was several miles away, and when her father couldn't pick her up, she took the bus home.

The strip mall offered a few other shops. There were a shoe store, an electronics store, a supermarket, and a recently opened jewelry store. When the girls saw Veronica approaching them, they knew there was only one reason she'd be there, and it certainly wasn't to meet them—let alone catch the bus.

"Have you come to buy a gold trinket to soothe yourself after that trying visit to Pine Hollow?" Stevie taunted. Veronica was such an easy target for her teasing that it was almost embarrassing, but she was so full of herself that Stevie simply couldn't resist.

"You can be as snide as you want," Veronica answered. "But the next time Red neglects Belle or Starlight—well, I just want to hear what you have to say to Max about it!"

"Are you going into Baubles and Bangles?" Lisa asked, hoping to steer the conversation in a more neutral direction. That was the jewelry store behind them.

"Yes," Veronica said. "I need a new stock pin for the next time Danny and I are in a show. It's hardly suitable to be in the winner's circle with that old thing I've got now. It got bent when I was thrown—you remember the time Red startled Danny when we were warming up at the show?"

They did remember, but it had hardly been Red's fault that Danny had been allowed to approach the jump too fast. Veronica had yanked on the reins to slow him just when she should have been letting him jump.

"One certainly can't show with a bent pin," Stevie agreed. Then she had another idea. "Say, you know, I was looking through the Cross County catalog last night, and they have some really pretty jewelry, including a great collection of stock pins. . . ."

"Gold?"

"Of course," said Stevie.

"Eighteen-karat?"

"No, I think they're fourteen," said Stevie.

Veronica's response was a withering look. "Inferior quality," she said. "Just like the help at the stable."

"What do you mean by that?" Carole asked, unable to resist.

"As if you didn't know, or maybe you don't because you've grown to expect second-rate service." Veronica paused for effect. "Anyway, just to alert you, once again, Red failed to secure the latch on Danny's stall."

"But didn't you put Danny in there yourself?" Carole asked, recalling specifically that she'd seen Veronica do so.

"Well, yes, but it was certainly Red's responsibility to check to see that it was latched after I left, and he clearly never got around to it. Do you know what might have happened if I hadn't gone back to see that he'd done his job?"

"Yes, of course I know," said Carole, horrified that Veronica would take such a terrible risk with such a valuable horse. "Your horse might have walked right out of his stall and into all kinds of danger. What were you thinking?"

"Me? Red is the one who failed here," said Veronica. "He's the stable hand, isn't he?"

"Stable hand yes, personal servant no," said Stevie.

"Oh, look!" Veronica said. "The store is about to close. I'd better hurry!" With that, she left the three girls standing at the bus stop.

"Only Veronica," Lisa said.

"Can you imagine intentionally putting your horse at risk in order to test Red's skills as a stable hand?" Carole asked, still stunned.

"There are two things about Veronica," Stevie said. "One is that nothing is ever her fault, and the other is that there is no depth to which she will not sink."

"And all of that makes her a constant source of entertainment for us," Lisa added.

"And work for Red," said Carole.

Just then Carole's bus pulled up to the stop in the parking lot. The girls hastily made arrangements to meet at Pine Hollow after school the next day. They had their work cut out for them if they wanted to convince Max that Paul Fredericks was right and that they'd do a fine job as Honey-Pie's primary caretakers.

48

STEVIE SPOTTED HER friends at Honey-Pie's stall as soon as she entered the stable the next afternoon.

"So, what can we do for her?" she asked eagerly.

"Well—" Carole began.

"Let me put it this way," Lisa said, cutting off what sounded as if it might be a long, involved answer to a simple horse question—Carole's specialty. "It's going to be hard to prove that we're experts at taking care of a horse that needs as little care as this old gal."

"I couldn't have said it better," Carole agreed, aware of, and amused by, Lisa's tactic. "Red cleaned out her stall, gave her fresh hay and water, and that's about it."

"We could turn her out into her paddock," Stevie said.

"If she hasn't already been out too much," said Carole.

"I'll check," said Lisa, and went out in search of Red to make sure it would be okay to give Honey-Pie some fresh air.

Stevie patted the horse and gave her a bit of carrot while they waited.

"Red says okay," Lisa informed them.

Stevie opened the door to the little paddock while Carole stood aside, allowing the mare to pass her. Honey-Pie glanced at her, apparently assuring herself that Carole wasn't going to try the lead rope thing again, and trotted out into the paddock.

"Wow, that was a big job," Stevie teased. There was an edge to her comment, though, because none of them could figure out why Max seemed to doubt their ability to look after this horse.

"Well, if there's nothing more to do for Honey-Pie, perhaps we can do something for ourselves," Carole suggested. "Max left the low jumps up in the schooling ring, and that gives us a chance to work on jump form. Why don't we tack up and go have some fun?"

Lisa glanced across Honey-Pie's paddock to the schooling ring and saw that Carole was right. The whole ring was set up with eighteen-inch jumps. The jumps themselves would be no challenge for their horses to get over, and that would make it all the more important to work on their jumping style. One thing she'd learned in her relatively short time as a rider was that if she could do something perfectly when it was made easy for her, she'd be able to do it better when it was harder.

In fifteen minutes, the three girls were ready to begin. Carole went first. Her horse, Starlight, was a natural jumper, and she had learned a lot from him.

But this exercise was difficult for the bay gelding. He loved jumping so much that he tended to overjump—to begin too early or jump too high. In hunter-jumping, form was everything, and a horse that jumped four feet high to clear an eighteen-inch jump didn't have good form. Carole had to work hard to keep him from taking off too far from the little jumps.

Carole was annoyed with her performance. "Go ahead, Stevie, you show me how to do it."

"It's tougher than it looks, isn't it?" Stevie asked.

"For us, yes, but I bet you'll do better."

"Not likely," Stevie said modestly. It turned out that she was wrong, however. Belle and Stevie often worked together on dressage, a precise form of competitive riding in which every single move made a difference in the score. When Stevie held Belle back from jumping too early, Belle held back from jumping too high.

"Nicely done!" Carole said.

"You kept her on a tight rein, didn't you?" Lisa asked. "Was that why she did so well?"

51

"Partly," said Stevie. "Also, all my aids were given in very small doses—like, I only loosened the reins a little bit, leaned forward a small amount, and held her from her takeoff until the very last minute. Remember, a horse cannot see anything that is immediately in front of him and nearby, so he's relying on you to tell him about the jump. It becomes invisible at the most critical moment."

"Okay, I'll try now," said Lisa, although she wasn't confident that she'd have much success.

She nudged Prancer to a trot and then to a slow, even canter. She circled the ring once to be sure she and Prancer were in balance; then she opened her left rein a little bit to bring the mare in line with the first jump. Prancer, seeing the jump ahead, began to speed up. Lisa tightened up on the reins to make Prancer return to their earlier pace. Prancer obeyed. The jump wasn't high, but Prancer knew she had to get over it. She lunged toward it. Lisa didn't release the reins and allow her to make the jump until they were very close, less than two feet. Prancer got the message. She pushed off with her hind legs and responded with a gentle upward surge as Lisa leaned forward in the saddle and moved her hands up, relaxing the pull on the bit. Prancer cleared the low jump and landed smoothly.

"I did it!" Lisa said.

"Good form!" Carole complimented her.

"Well done," Stevie agreed.

The rest of the jumps seemed easy after that. Lisa was glad of the exercise. Sometimes the easiest-looking things were the hardest to do right.

As she drew Prancer over to the fence for the rest of the critique she knew she would get—and learn from— she glanced toward the driveway and saw a sports car pulling up in front of the barn. It was a black Jaguar.

"Hey, it's Mr. Call-me-Paul," said Stevie.

They watched as Paul Fredericks stepped out of the car, once again dressed for a country club. They expected to see him head into the stable to meet with Max, but they were wrong. He walked over to them.

"Hey, look at the three of you," he said brightly. "On horses!"

"That's what we do here," said Carole. "We ride horses."

"That is, we ride them when we're not looking after them," Lisa added.

"Well you seem to be riding them very well," he said.

The girls had done nothing but sit in their saddles since the car had come into the driveway. It was hard for Stevie to figure out how he'd decided they were riding well under the circumstances, but there seemed no reason to make an issue of it.

"Max is in the office," Carole said.

"I'll see him later, but I'd love to watch you all for a while—that is, if you don't mind."

"We don't mind, Mr. Fredericks," said Lisa.

"Please, call me Paul," he said.

"Uh, sure, Paul," said Lisa. She was uncomfortable with that, but she wasn't sure why. Perhaps it was because it seemed too familiar with someone who wasn't really a friend. She shrugged it off. If he wanted to be called Paul, she'd try to do it.

Carole began the round of jumps again, this time reining Starlight in as Stevie had done with Belle and getting respectable results.

"Better," Stevie said.

"Better? I thought she was fabulous!" Paul said. "Why, that horse jumped those fences as if they were nothing at all!"

"Those are only eighteen-inch fences," Lisa said. "They *are* almost nothing at all."

"Well, they sure look scary to me!" Paul said.

The girls took several more turns over the course, but it wasn't as much fun with Paul there admiring every single thing they did, error or not. He said "Wow" and applauded after every jump. It almost distracted the horses and certainly distracted Stevie, Lisa, and Carole.

Finally the horses were ready for a rest, and so were the girls.

"Would you like to see Honey-Pie?" Lisa suggested. "She's settled in nicely, and we let her out into her paddock before we came out here to ride."

"Sure," said Paul. "And maybe we can talk a bit about her care."

"Absolutely," Carole said enthusiastically. "We're working with Max and Red to see that she's well looked after—like all the horses here. As an older horse, and one that isn't being ridden, she needs a few special considerations. I spent some time last night researching the care of retired horses. I think we're all going to learn from Honey-Pie, and if love counts toward care—and I think it does—well, you can count on a healthy horse for a long time to come!"

Paul smiled weakly.

"Come on, Carole, I'll take Starlight to his stall for you," Stevie offered, thinking that if Paul could hear more about what Carole had learned from her research on Honey-Pie's behalf, he'd be all the happier that he was boarding the mare at Pine Hollow and might even put in another good word for them with Max.

It took only a few minutes to untack Belle and Starlight, and when Stevie returned, she found Carole deep into a discussion about feeding schedules. On his previous visit, Paul had noticed that Red was giving some of the other horses a grain ration, and he wondered why Honey-Pie wasn't getting one.

"Honey-Pie isn't as active as the other horses," Carole said. "She doesn't need the extra nutrients that are in the afternoon feeding. She'll get her grain in the morning, after she's had water and hay. She has access to water at all times and will get three or four feedings of hay every day on a schedule."

"I want her to get more grain," Paul said, sounding a little petulant.

"It wouldn't be good for her," said Carole, automatically taking the horse's side.

"Who's the better judge of that?" Paul asked, sounding almost angry. He calmed down right away, though. "I'm sure you girls know what you're doing, but I do want to be sure the horse gets the kind of care Aunt Emma would have demanded for her, and I'm sure Aunt Emma used to give her grain twice a day. It's not a good idea to change her schedule abruptly, is it?"

"No, it isn't," Carole agreed.

"And you wouldn't want to do anything that was bad for good old Honey-Pie, now, would you?"

"No, we wouldn't," Carole agreed.

"You know what I think?" Paul asked. The girls asked him what, although they were beginning to suspect that they didn't care what he thought.

"Well, I think the people who take the very best care of Honey-Pie at Pine Hollow deserve some sort of treat."

"Treats are good," Stevie agreed, wondering what he was leading up to. She didn't have long to wait.

"How would you three—I mean, if you take good care of Honey-Pie and she does as well here as I know she will when you do what I tell you—like to come for a ride on my yacht? We could spend a whole day at sea."

"Like, take a picnic?" Lisa asked.

"No need to bring anything at all," Paul said. "I'd have my cook prepare something delicious for us. Whatever you want, really."

"Um, Mr. Fredericks . . . ," Carole began.

"Please call me Paul."

"Right, um, Paul," she continued. "We're going to look after Honey-Pie because it's the right thing to do. You don't have to pay us or anything."

"It's not payment," Paul said. "It's just a way of saying thank you."

"Well, please wait until you have something to thank us for," Lisa told him.

"I'm sure it won't be long before that happens," said Paul. All three girls were a little surprised by the apparent smugness in his voice. "And I know it's what my aunt Emma would have wanted me to do for you."

"Thanks, Paul," said Stevie. "That's something to look forward to."

"Oh, look, here comes Max," said Carole, spotting

him on the way out of his office. "I'm sure you want to talk with him, right?"

Paul glanced at his watch. "No, I don't really have time to see him now. I'll talk to him later. Besides, it was you three I really wanted to see. Thanks for the great jumping demonstration and, most especially, for looking after sweet old Honey-Pie."

"You're welcome on both counts," Stevie said.

"Well, ahoy, mateys!" he declared, waving as he slipped out the back door, through the schooling ring, and back to his car.

The girls exchanged glances.

"Was that weird or what?" Stevie asked.

"Definitely," Lisa agreed.

"And I don't care what he says. If Aunt Emma—whoever she is—er, was—loved Honey-Pie, she'd know that a retired horse shouldn't get two rations of grain a day."

"And anyone who tries to make me overfeed this sweet mare is going to have to walk the plank!" Carole pronounced.

"A day on his yacht!" Stevie said. "Do you believe it?"

"It might be fun—" Lisa said.

"Except for one thing," said Stevie.

"Right. He'd be there, good old Mr. Call-me-Paul."

"CAROLE, YOU WERE letting Starlight get away with murder in class today," Max Regnery said at the end of the flat class that followed their Pony Club meeting the next Saturday.

Carole cringed, but she wasn't the only one getting criticism. "Lisa, you must remember your basic aids," Max went on. "If you don't master the basics, you'll never accomplish any worthwhile goals." Lisa flushed with embarrassment at the sharpness of his words.

"And *Stevie*." Max didn't even continue. His irritation with Stevie was so apparent that there wasn't any need for him to say more. He turned and left the three girls holding their horses while he went to tend to some of the other riders.

"He is so angry with us!" Stevie said.

"What did we do wrong?" Lisa asked.

"Maybe we were just being sloppy in class?" Carole suggested. "I mean, he's right. Starlight was misbehaving and I wasn't controlling him properly."

"And I let my heels come up and my elbows were flopping," Lisa said.

"I couldn't help it if Veronica was being so annoying that I just had to hide her bridle before class," said Stevie.

"Well, it did delay the class for ten minutes while we all looked for it," Lisa reminded her.

"Still, it *was* Veronica," Stevie protested. "But now we have to do some wonderful things to make Max like us again."

"And trust us," Lisa added.

"Let's longe Honey-Pie," Carole suggested.

"Does she need it?" Lisa asked.

"Every horse needs it," Carole reminded her. "And Honey-Pie's been in her box stall and that little paddock all week. I'm sure she's ready for some nice stretching exercises, and since we can't ride her, the best way to do that is to longe her."

"Okay," said Lisa. "And then, after we've done that, let's give our own horses some nice stretching exercises, too."

60

"Like, for instance, a trail ride?" Stevie asked.

"Like, for instance, exactly," said Lisa.

The deal was struck. All three girls returned their horses to their stalls, and Carole brought the longeing tack from the storage room.

The term *longeing*—usually pronounced like *lunging*—came from the French word for "long," and longeing was done with long tack. The horse was fitted with a set of equipment that included a saddlelike pad, a bridle, and a very long rein, designed to be used from one side of the horse by someone in the center of a ring. It made it look as if the horse were on a leash, but the bridle had a bit and the horse could be controlled with that and with the aid of a long whip. Longeing could be used for many things. For example, it allowed a rider to watch her own horse in particular gaits. And in the case of a horse that couldn't be under saddle for whatever reason, it was a very good way of seeing to it that the horse got enough exercise.

Carole took the longe line and the whip. She and Lisa stood in the middle of the ring and began exercising Honey-Pie, who responded immediately to Carole's long-distance aids.

"She loves it, doesn't she?" Lisa asked, watching the horse closely.

"I think so," Carole said. Honey-Pie wasn't going

61

fast—just moving at an extended walk—but already it was clear that she was happy to be exercising. Her ears were perked straight up, flicking this way and that—she was alert to everything around her. She held her head high, and her stride was elegantly smooth.

Stevie was perched on the top of the rail fence, flipping through the Cross County Tack Shop catalog while keeping an eye on the doings in the ring. It was good to see Honey-Pie respond so well to the longeing.

"I bet she's done this a lot," said Stevie. "Or else she's just taking to it naturally."

"I don't know," Carole said. "This is a horse that was ridden a lot and loved it. I mean, she loves people. Her previous owner—I guess that must have been Aunt Emma—was really lucky. I wish we could ride her, too."

"Let's see how she trots," Lisa suggested.

Carole gave the mare a signal and Honey-Pie shifted smoothly into the faster gait.

Stevie become aware that they had company only when she felt the fence move a bit—someone was climbing it. She turned to see who was joining her. It was Paul Fredericks.

"Hi, Sammy," he said.

"Stevie," she corrected him.

"I'm sorry. Right church, wrong pew, huh?"

"Sort of. It's short for Stephanie," she told him.

"Oh, of course. That makes sense." He pulled himself up over the top rail and settled awkwardly next to Stevie. "What are they doing?" he asked, looking into the ring.

Stevie explained what longeing was and why they were doing it. Paul watched for a while.

Stevie was uncomfortably aware of his presence. It wasn't that he was doing anything wrong or bad. He just didn't belong there. Once again, he was dressed in very expensive clothes. Lisa would have been able to tell her the brand names and Veronica would have been able to pinpoint the price, but Stevie didn't need any help to know that wool slacks, cashmere sweaters, and tassel loafers had no business sitting on a rail fence in a stable yard.

"Would you like me to get you a chair or something?" Stevie offered. "I mean, those clothes . . ."

"Nah, I'm fine," Paul said. "I don't care if something happens to these old things. I just want to be sure Honey-Pie's okay."

"Honey-Pie's fine," Stevie assured him.

"Well, you know, I only want the best for her," Paul said.

"We know. And that's what she's getting."

Wanting the best for a horse made Stevie think of the catalog in her hand. Although she and her friends had been working hard to raise money for CARL by getting people to order from Cross County Tack, the pennies were mounting up a lot faster than the dollars, and they had a long way to go. It occurred to Stevie that someone who thought of expensive clothes as "these old things" might be in the market for some goods for his horse.

"You know," Stevie began, "I've been looking over Honey-Pie's equipment, and although she's got most of what she needs, she could use a few items. Perhaps you'd like to consider, say, um, a new blanket. Look, there's one in this catalog."

She showed Paul a lovely dark green blanket that would look good on Honey-Pie, explaining that anything he ordered would help CARL buy a horse van.

"She's got a blanket, doesn't she?" he asked.

"Yes, but it's old and it's light. She'd do well to have something warmer for the winter, especially when she's not being ridden. If she got too cold, it could cause all kinds of problems."

Stevie would have loved to persuade Paul to buy an expensive blanket, but she wasn't lying. Honey-Pie's blanket was a summer-weight one, and she would need something warmer, though Max would surely supply one if she didn't have her own.

"She can make do," Paul said, shrugging off Stevie's suggestion. "But since it's all for a good cause, could I make a donation?"

"Oh, of course!" Stevie said, delighted. She hadn't even thought of that possibility.

Paul shifted his weight to reach the wallet in his back pocket. Like everything he wore and everything about him, it was clearly expensive—alligator skin, shiny, and new. Veronica would have known for sure, but the wallet alone must have been worth a significant percent of their fund-raising goal.

"Our goal is to raise five hundred dollars," Stevie said, wondering how much he might consider contributing.

"Well, I certainly want to be a part of something that's going to mean so much to the horses in this county," he said, reaching into his wallet.

Stevie could feel her heart quicken. She kept her eyes off Paul's fingers as they shuffled among the sheaf of bills in the wallet. It would be rude to stare. She just smiled and waited, accepting the two bills he pressed into her hands.

"Thanks so much," she said sincerely. "You can't imagine what this is going to mean."

"I'm glad to help, in my own small way," Paul said.

Stevie put the bills into her pocket. She wasn't worried for a second that she would leave them there. She was proud of herself for telling Paul about the fundraising drive and felt real joy that he'd made a contribution to their cause. Maybe he didn't know much about looking after Honey-Pie, but he cared, and that mattered. And he'd contributed, and that mattered more.

"Look at this, uh, Paul," Carole called out to him. She was as uncomfortable as her friends calling the man by his first name. "Do you see how happy Honey-Pie is?"

"Oh, sure, I can tell right away," he said, though Stevie didn't think he really knew when a horse was content. "Why don't you try to get her to trot?" he asked.

"She is trotting," Carole said.

"Doesn't look very fast to me," said Paul. "I thought trotting was faster than that."

"Well, trotting isn't the speed, it's the gait," Carole said.

"Trotting is definitely faster than that," said Paul.

"Not really," Stevie said. It was easier for her to explain because she was sitting next to him. "See, trotting is a two-beat gait. The legs on opposite corners of the horse go together in a trot. Left fore, right rear are together; right fore, left rear are together."

"Shouldn't she be going faster?" he insisted to Carole in spite of Stevie's explanation.

"I guess she's warm enough," Carole said. She signaled Honey-Pie for a canter. Honey-Pie responded immediately.

"Now she's galloping, right?" Paul asked Carole.

"No, this is a canter," Carole called back.

"A canter is a three-beat gait," Stevie said, ready to explain if necessary. It wasn't necessary, or at least there wasn't any point in it because Paul wasn't listening. He seemed interested simply in getting the horse to go as fast as possible.

"Make her gallop, then," he ordered.

"I can't, really," Carole said.

"Just hit her with the whip!" he commanded.

"No, that's not the reason Carole won't gallop her," Stevie said, but it was clear Paul still wasn't listening. He apparently didn't want to hear about the dangers of overworking a sedentary horse on a longe line.

"You said she was obedient. She'll gallop for you if you whip her," Paul repeated, calling out to Carole.

Carole couldn't understand why Stevie wasn't explaining the situation better. True, Carole was known for giving explanations that were too long and complicated, but Stevie ought to be able to make it clear that Honey-Pie's first workout shouldn't strain her muscles. She brought the horse back down to an easy walk, handed the longe line to Lisa, and went over to talk to Paul herself.

"Gee, Mr. Fredericks—" she began.

"Call me Paul," he said automatically.

"Well, it's not a good idea to take a horse—an older horse at that—who's been in a small enclosure like Honey-Pie's paddock and make her go too fast all at once. There's no benefit to it at all, and there could be some harm. Now, if she were out in a field and decided on her own to gallop somewhere, well, that would be another thing altogether. See, a horse's muscles are very much like a human's, but the leg muscles can be quite fragile. As you can see, the horse's hind legs are substantial, but the forelegs are relatively slender, yet they support more than half of the horse's weight."

Stevie knew what was coming. It was Carole's forty-five-minute talk on horse anatomy. Stevie wanted to do something to stop her friend, but it turned out to be unnecessary because they were interrupted by Veronica.

"What are you doing taking up the entire ring with that old nag?" Veronica asked Lisa in her usual demanding tone.

"We're longeing her," Lisa answered, as if it were necessary to tell Veronica what was going on.

"Well, I want a chance to work with Danny on some exercises my private jump instructor recommended. Red will have him tacked up in ten minutes, and I hope you'll be done with Honey-Pie"—she said the name as if she were holding it at arm's length—"by then. See that you are, all right?"

"Perhaps you'd like to clear that with Mr. Fredericks?" Lisa said, nodding toward Paul, Carole, and Stevie.

Veronica had a sudden personality change. Since Stevie, Lisa, and Carole couldn't stand any of her personalities, it didn't make the slightest difference to them. Paul, on the other hand, seemed quite charmed.

"Oh! Why, hello! It's so nice to see you," said Veronica.

"Who else was she expecting to have arrived in a Jaguar?" Stevie whispered to Carole. Veronica had not acknowledged the existence of the other two girls.

"Why, that sweet old horse of yours must be exhausted by now," Veronica said. "Why don't you tell the hands to put her away? I'm planning to ride my Thoroughbred out here in a few minutes. Perhaps you'd like a chance to see a real horse in action?"

Paul climbed down from the fence. "No thanks. I think I've seen enough horse action for one day." He turned to Stevie and Carole. "Thanks, and keep up the good work with Honey-Pie, okay?"

"Okay," Stevie said. Carole started to suggest talking about an exercise schedule for the mare, but Paul wasn't paying attention. He just headed directly to his car. Carole had also wanted to let him know where to find Max so that the two men could talk about the mare's care, but before the words were out of her mouth, Paul had the engine purring and was pulling out of Pine Hollow's driveway.

"Strange," Stevie said. Lisa brought Honey-Pie to a halt and drew in the longe line. The horse came over to her willingly, as she did everything.

"Okay, girl, time to get back to your stall."

"Most important, it's time for our trail ride," Carole said.

"Last one tacked up is a rotten egg," Stevie challenged.

As far as Stevie was concerned, there was nothing in the world nicer than seeing the woods, hills, rocks, trees, and streams of Willow Creek, Virginia, from the back of her horse. She loved trail rides. And even better, her two best friends did, too.

The three of them trotted briskly along the trail they knew well, Carole first, then Lisa, then Stevie at the rear. They didn't have to talk about where they were riding. They were going to their favorite place: the creek. Carole was securing Starlight's reins to a bush and Lisa was dismounting by the time Stevie joined them.

"That was great!" Stevie said, swinging her leg over Belle's back and lowering herself to the ground.

71

"It always is," Lisa agreed.

"Nothing cures what ails you like a ride in the woods," said Carole, heading for the rock where they could dangle their feet in the water—if it wasn't too cold.

One touch of the water told Carole that it was too cold, but that didn't mean they couldn't enjoy a chat while they sat together in the sunshine.

"And a lot ails us," Carole said, finishing her thought.

"Yeah, like how we can convince Max we're worthy to look after Honey-Pie the way Paul said we should," said Lisa.

"But even more, like what's up with Call-me-Paul," Carole said. "Imagine wanting to get a horse who's been cooped up in a stall to gallop on a longe line. That's weird."

"*He's* a little weird, if you ask me," said Lisa.

"Oh, don't be too hasty," Stevie said, recalling his donation to CARL for the horse trailer. "He didn't want to buy anything for Honey-Pie, but he gave me money."

"Great!" said Carole.

"How much?" asked Lisa, ever the practical member of the group.

"Actually, I don't know," Stevie said. "It seemed rude to look while he went through his wallet, so I just took the bills and said thank you."

"And where did you put them?" Lisa asked.

"In my pocket," said Stevie.

"So?"

Stevie shifted her weight and reached into her pocket. She could feel the money there. She thought about the Jaguar, the Armani slacks, the Gucci shoes, the alligator wallet. Paul Fredericks was a rich man. He was generous, too. He'd offered to take her and her friends out on his yacht. Generous people made generous donations. Once again, Stevie was pleased that she'd thought to ask him to help with the CARL project.

The money had slipped down into the bottom of her pocket. She had to stand up to fish it out. She felt the paper, encircled it with her fingers, and pulled it out, holding it out to her friends.

There in her hands lay two slightly wrinkled one-dollar bills.

"Two bucks? That's it?" Stevie said incredulously.

"There must be more," Lisa said logically.

"No, there isn't," Stevie said, but she checked the pocket again, and then she checked all her other pockets. No, there was no mistake. Generous, wealthy, kind, horse-loving Paul Fredericks had given her two dollars. Period.

"Definitely weird," said Carole.

"There's something awfully strange going on here," Stevie said.

"Very strange," Carole agreed. "But we have to keep ourselves focused. See, it's easy to get distracted by Jaguars and pinstripe suits, but the only thing that really matters is that sweet horse. We just have to keep doing our job, take the best possible care of Honey-Pie, and wait for Max to figure out that we know what we're doing."

"Deal," said Lisa, holding up her hand. Stevie and Carole hit it and the deal was sealed.

Soon it was time for the girls to get back to Pine Hollow. It had been a long day already with their Pony Club meeting, the class, longeing Honey-Pie, collecting two whole dollars for CARL, and their trail ride. They remounted and had a leisurely walk through the woods back to the stable.

One good part of the day wasn't over yet. Since it was a Saturday, they'd planned to spend the night together, and Stevie's parents had given them permission to have a sleepover at her house.

One thing they agreed on as they rode back to Pine Hollow was that they wanted to talk to Max before they left for the day and make a list of the things he thought they ought to be doing with Honey-Pie. As soon as they'd bedded their own horses for the night, Stevie got out her notebook and the three girls headed for Max's office.

They stopped before they reached the door, however. There was a conversation going on, and it was a heated one. Normally Max closed his office door when he was angry, but it wasn't Max who was angry. It was Benjamin Stookey.

"Fredericks tells me you're letting those three little girls act as Honey-Pie's exclusive caretakers. I want to remind you, Regnery, that you are being paid handsomely to give that horse first-class treatment, and if anything happens to her . . ."

Stevie, Lisa, and Carole flattened themselves against the wall. They didn't want to miss a word, but they also didn't want Max to know they were there.

". . . Honey-Pie's primary caretakers should not be three adolescents! There are fiduciary issues here that I cannot overlook, and as the court-appointed guardian . . ."

He went on. Words and phrases like *co-beneficiary* and *residual beneficiary* poured out of his mouth, leaving three heads shaking in the hallway. They would have loved to see Max's response. Then they heard it.

"Mr. Stookey, I have told both you and Mr. Fredericks that every single horse in this stable gets excellent care and much of that excellent care comes from my fine young students. I oversee their work when necessary, but there isn't a rider here who doesn't know how to take care of a sweet horse like Honey-Pie. I assure you, she's getting first-class care, and if your fiduciary issues and residual beneficiaries are not satisfied, perhaps you'd better find another stable—"

"You—You were highly recommended," Mr. Stookey stammered.

"And for good reason!" Max boomed.

The girls didn't have to see Max's face to know what it looked like. Max was often annoyed, but he rarely lost his temper. On the occasions when he did, however, it was memorable. His face turned red and his glare was icy. The three friends were very glad indeed that they weren't the recipients of his glare at that moment.

"I guess maybe I've overreacted," Mr. Stookey said, backing down quickly.

"I think perhaps you did," said Max, lowering his voice and trying to be polite. "But let me assure you that if at any time you find that anyone here has mistreated Honey-Pie, I'll be the first person to help you find another stable for her. I wouldn't tolerate mistreatment any more than you would."

"I'm sure you wouldn't," Mr. Stookey said. "Well, you know, this is a totally awkward situation."

"The awkward situation has nothing to do with me," Max said. "My job is to look after the horse the way Mrs. Fredericks would have done herself. The only thing I'd

76

recommend that you're not doing is to let her be ridden a couple of times a week."

"Emma was the only person who ever rode her," said Mr. Stookey. "I can't believe that it would be good to have total strangers ride her."

"Limiting her exercise may not be good for her, either," said Max. "Nevertheless, the orders are clear. She won't be ridden. I do think I'll suggest that some of my students longe her from time to time."

"Longe? That sounds dangerous!"

While Max explained what it meant, the girls looked at one another and exchanged victorious grins. They'd thought of that without any help or instruction from Max. He'd be pleased to know she'd had a half hour on the longe line that afternoon. At least, they thought he'd be pleased. How could it be that a few days before, he'd told Paul he wasn't so sure they could do all the work, and now here he was telling Mr. Stookey they knew everything there was to know? Things were going from weird to weirder.

A few minutes later, a quiet and humbled Benjamin Stookey slunk out of Max's office and headed for his Volvo. He never even glanced at the three girls still pinned to the wall.

The girls were about to unpin themselves when another person didn't notice they were there.

Veronica diAngelo swept past them, crying, "Max!"

"This is not a good—"

"Max! It's Danny! He's *gone!*"

"What do you mean, gone?"

"Not there. Gone. Empty stall. Flown the coop! It's Red, you know. He left the stall unlatched again and Danny—everybody knows that he's curious and wanders. He left. Gone. It's Red's responsibility. I've told you repeatedly that that man doesn't know the first thing—"

"Red's—*Red's* responsibility?" Max stammered. For the second time in as many minutes, Stevie, Lisa, and Carole were hearing Max's fury.

"That horse belongs to *you!*" Max's voice thundered out of his office. "*You* were riding him. *You* are responsible for seeing that he's secure in his stall!"

"I told Red to look after him!" Veronica said, but her voice was quieter than before. Her arguments weren't working and she was beginning to realize it.

"And I told you before that you cannot be careless with the latch on Danny's stall. This is inexcusable, Veronica. Danny is a strong and headstrong horse. There's no telling where he's going to go and what kind of trouble he can get into. The fields and woods around here are filled with hazards for a horse like Danny. You may think it's okay to risk your Thoroughbred's health—or even his life—to make a stupid point with Red, but it's not. Latching your horse's stall door is your job. Not anybody else's. If he comes back here—and I suppose he will, though why he'd want to return to your care is beyond me—you will remain solely responsible for his care.

"Now, since, in all likelihood, Danny has headed for the woods, probably toward the creek, perhaps you'd like to rent a horse from the stable to see if you might be able to find him. I'm sure a horse could be found for you."

"Well, I, uh—just one of the stable horses?"

It was totally typical of Veronica to despise the idea of riding just any horse.

"Danny isn't available," Max said, the anger dripping from his voice.

"But Max, shouldn't Red—"

"No!" he shouted. "Danny is your horse. This is your fault, and it's your responsibility to fix it. Now go. Solve the problem!"

Max slammed his office door behind Veronica.

Veronica stomped off down the hall, pulling a sleek cell phone out of her jacket pocket. Nobody had to tell Stevie, Lisa, and Carole what she was up to. She was calling her father.

By the time The Saddle Club had changed out of

their riding clothes and picked up their overnight bags to leave for Stevie's house, Veronica had solved the problem at least as far as she was concerned. She had walked into the locker area and headed straight for the bulletin board. There she posted a note:

Missing: Valuable Thoroughbred Horse. "Go For Blue," called Danny. $1,000 reward for anyone who brings him back to Pine Hollow unharmed.

Once the note was pinned to the board, Veronica marched out of the room without saying a word to The Saddle Club.

Stevie shook her head. "Only Veronica would think money could make up for carelessness," she observed.

"Her parents, too, I guess," Lisa said.

"A lesson she learned well at her father's knee," said Carole.

9

LISA ALWAYS ENJOYED a meal with the Lakes because it was so unlike anything that ever happened at her house. Dinner in the Lake house was managed mayhem. Amid shouts and playful teasing, Mrs. Lake managed to put all the food on the table with the help of an assigned child, and Mr. Lake managed to serve it up with the help of another assigned child. That night, Alex was carrying food out of the kitchen while enjoying a heated argument with Chad about whether the Willow Creek High School basketball team had a snowball's chance in July of beating Cross County. Michael was talking with his mother about the history of protest in the United States, centering on the Vietnam era, and Stevie was trying to get her father to tell her what *fiduciary responsibility* meant while she doled out the plates he filled.

Carole and Lisa watched and listened, absorbing. Lisa felt a little like someone trying to catch a bus that was already moving. Eventually she might learn how fast to run and how firmly to grab, but for now it seemed safer to stand on the curb and wait for the next bus.

"That guy can't rebound for beans!"

"But if the country was wrong, why were some people fighting the war at all?"

"It's a passing game!"

"Civil disobedience . . ."

"Foul shots! He's three for fourteen!"

"*Fidoosh*, something like that. It sure sounded like a lawyer's word to me."

"Ah, *fiduciary*!"

"Yeah, that's it!" Stevie almost dropped the plate she was holding in front of Chad. It landed with such a loud noise that Chad himself was momentarily silenced.

"What does it mean?" Carole piped up.

"It has to do with trusts," said Mr. Lake.

"Huh?" Stevie never minded letting on that she was confused.

"The person who is in charge of a trust—"

"What's a trust?"

"It can be a lot of things, but mostly it has to do with money that's being held and managed for someone else. When there's a trust, the person in charge is a trustee and has fiduciary responsibility. In other words, they are accountable. It might be helpful if you know that it comes from the Latin word—"

"*Semper Fi!*" said Carole. "It's the Marines' motto."

"Exactly," said Mr. Lake. "Only it's actually *Semper Fidelis—fi* is a shortened version. Anyway, what *Fidelis* means, literally, is 'faithful.' *Semper* means 'always,' so the Marine Corps motto means 'always faithful.' A fiduciary must be faithful to the terms of the trust. Does that answer your question?" he asked.

"What does that have to do with horses?" Lisa asked.

By then all the plates had been filled and everyone was seated. The noise abated as Stevie's brothers concentrated on eating; so The Saddle Club had Mr. and Mrs. Lake's full attention.

"It doesn't have anything to do with horses, as far as I know," Mr. Lake told her.

Stevie looked at the notebook where she'd jotted down the confusing words Mr. Stookey had used in his conversation with Max. She'd intended to use the pad to write down all the things Max wanted the girls to do with Honey-Pie. Instead, she'd written *fiduciary responsibility*, though she was sure she'd spelled it wrong. Next to that was another confusing term.

"What's a residual beneficiary, then?" she asked.

"Sometimes when someone dies, they leave their money and goods directly to someone else—to their children, for example. When the money is left in a trust, if the person who's supposed to benefit from the trust dies, the money goes to the residual beneficiary—"

"Like the next person on the list?" Lisa asked.

"I'm not sure most lawyers would let you put it that way, but it's close enough."

"And what does that have to do with horses?" Carole asked.

"Nothing," said Mr. Lake. He was looking more and more confused by the girls' questions. "What is all this about?"

"Well, there's this guy," Stevie began.

"And this horse," said Carole.

"The guy is Benjamin Stookey," said Stevie.

"And there's this other guy named Paul Fredericks," said Lisa.

"Honey-Pie?" asked Mrs. Lake. "Is she at Pine Hollow?"

Stevie, Lisa, and Carole looked at her in astonishment. How on earth could she know? Then they looked at Mr. Lake. He was laughing.

"What's the joke?" Stevie asked.

"Oh, boy!" he said. "Old Emma really did it, didn't she?"

Mrs. Lake laughed, too.

"What's going on?" Carole asked Lisa.

"Oh, it's the talk of wills and trusts departments everywhere in Virginia!" Mr. Lake said, still laughing.

"So?" Stevie crossed her arms over her chest and waited impatiently for more information.

By then even her brothers were interested. All six of the kids at the table wanted to be in on the joke.

"You tell," said Mr. Lake.

"No, you tell," said Mrs. Lake. "You went to law school with Ben."

"Okay," Mr. Lake agreed. He took a drink of water and sat back in his chair. "This is all about Emma Fredericks," he began.

"Aunt Emma?" Lisa asked.

"Is that what Paul calls her? I guess so," Mr. Lake said. "Well, she was a strange old gal, that's for sure. She was married to Bart Fredericks. He was a schemer and a dreamer, and in his lifetime he went through about six fortunes. The world never knew whether he'd just lost a million dollars or earned it or was somewhere in between, but it was a sure thing that whatever he had, he wasn't going to keep it for long. When he died, he had lost it. He left Emma absolutely nothing. Or almost nothing. Turns out he'd owned a portion of a retired racehorse, and that racehorse happened to be a mare. That mare just happened to be in foal. And under Bart Fredericks's will, Emma inherited the foal.

"Emma took that foal in. At the time, she was living in a trailer and had a tiny yard where the foal, a filly she named Honey-Pie, lived. She raised that horse as if it were a puppy, playing with it and loving it. It can't have been easy for her, either. She had to work hard enough to feed herself—she and Bart never had children—and she also had to feed the horse. As some people in this room know, caring for a horse is a very expensive prospect.

"Anyway, eventually the mare got old enough to train and ride, and that just brought the two of them closer, and when she was fully mature, Emma began breeding her.

"It turned out that Honey-Pie was the best investment Bart ever made. As a riding horse, she wasn't worth much, but as a breeder, she was valuable. A number of Honey-Pie's foals became prizewinners, and she was sought after as a broodmare. Emma got a lot of offers for Honey-Pie, but she wouldn't consider selling. Instead she made a nice living on the foaling fees.

"But she also invested her money, very wisely, and before she knew it, Emma was able to move out of the trailer park and into a nice house, then a nicer house, and then a mansion. When the old girl died, she was worth almost three million dollars. It was like a joke on everybody who'd ever laughed at Bart. But the bigger joke was still to come.

"Are you sure you don't want to tell this part?" Mr. Lake asked his wife. "I mean, you do more will and trust work than I do."

"Keep going," said Mrs. Lake. "I'm enjoying eating."

"Okay, so Emma and Bart never had any children. All of Emma's family was gone. The only one left who was related to either of them was a nephew on Bart's side."

"Paul?" Carole asked.

"Paul," Mr. Lake confirmed. "Paul figured he was going to get every penny. While Emma was lingering on life support, he'd sold his own little house and was totally prepared to move into her house. He'd opened accounts at all the fancy stores in downtown Washington, and he'd put a down payment on some kind of—"

"Yacht!" Stevie supplied.

"Exactly," said her father. "And a—"

"Jaguar!" said Carole.

"I guess. I just heard it was a sports car. Anyway, when Emma died and the will was read, Paul was in for a big surprise. Ben Stookey was her attorney, and I heard he'd done everything he could to talk her out of it, but he couldn't. She left Paul a portion of her estate. There are rumors, but you never know. The rumors say it was about two hundred fifty thousand dollars. The rest of it she left in trust, with Ben as the trustee. For Honey-Pie."

"The million-dollar horse!" said Carole, understanding for the first time.

"A good deal more than that," said Mr. Lake. "Estimates—and, again, this is just rumor—are that the horse is worth about two and a half million dollars."

"And Paul?"

"He spent every penny he had even before he had it. Paul is in deep debt."

"So, why doesn't he sell the yacht and car and stuff?" Stevie asked.

"Ah, there comes the residual beneficiary stuff. Paul will get most of Emma's money eventually. When Honey-Pie dies."

Stevie's mind was working so fast her mouth didn't have a chance to catch up. Everything was becoming clear. Neither Ben nor Paul knew the first thing about horses—except that Paul seemed to know enough to know what wasn't good for Honey-Pie. He wanted the mare dead, and he thought The Saddle Club could make that happen for him!

"Uh, may we please be excused?" she asked. Before her parents could even answer, the girls were taking their plates out to the kitchen. They needed to talk.

"I CAN'T BELIEVE Max would do that to us," said Stevie. "Doesn't he trust us enough to tell us what's going on?"

"Maybe he thought it was just our business to look after Honey-Pie," Lisa said. "It doesn't matter what her bank account is. We'd take care of her just the same."

"But the problem is that he didn't warn us about Paul. All we heard was that he was hinting to Paul that *we* weren't trustworthy," Carole said.

"But I guess what he was thinking was that we were totally trustworthy, right?" Lisa asked.

It was Sunday morning and the girls were walking toward Pine Hollow. They'd been talking about the same thing since dinner the night before and they were fairly sure they understood two things now: Number one was that Paul Fredericks did not have Honey-Pie's best interests at heart, and number two was that they did.

"Isn't that will too weird?" Stevie asked.

"I like the idea of leaving a lot of money to a horse," Carole said.

"What can a horse do with two million dollars?" Lisa asked sensibly.

"I guess I didn't say that right. I like the idea of leaving money so that a lot of horses can be helped," Carole corrected herself. "If I had two million dollars and nobody but a useless nephew to give it to, I'd give it to charity."

"I can change my name to Charity if you'd like," Stevie offered. "Just let me know when you get the two million bucks, okay?"

"Ha ha," said Carole.

The girls opened the door to the stable and walked in.

"If Max is in his office, I think we should talk with him," Lisa said. "He should know that we know about Honey-Pie, and he should also know that Paul's been lurking around here trying to talk us into doing bad things for her."

"Max knows we'd never do those things!" Carole said.

"Right, but he may not know that Paul's been trying to talk us into doing them—like overfeeding her and overexercising her."

The girls turned toward the stable office, but the door was closed. It was a sure sign that no one was welcome to knock or come in.

But the door wasn't closed tightly and, standing right outside it as they were, it was impossible for The Saddle Club not to hear what was going on.

"It is clear from what our daughter says that the staff here is inadequate to take care of . . ."

No question whose voice that was. Nobody but a diAngelo would speak to Max that way. It had to be Veronica's father. Her mother was there, too.

"She said that boy, Red Something—"

"O'Malley," Max supplied.

". . . just doesn't care about the horses the way he ought to. I mean, we know you don't have any other particularly valuable horses here, but if you want to have any in the future, perhaps you'll have to consider hiring a more professional staff."

There was a pause. Outside the office door, the girls didn't move. They weren't going to miss a second of this. They knew what was going on. Max was taking a deep breath and thinking about what he was going to say.

"Mr. and Mrs. diAngelo," he began. "I appreciate the fact that you have heard everything that happened from Veronica's point of view. Perhaps there were one or two things that she failed to mention to you."

It was music to the girls' ears to hear Max list the things Veronica had left out, like that it wasn't Red's job to latch the stable door, that Veronica frequently treated him as if he were her personal servant, that every other rider in the stable understood that it was his or her own job to look after his or her horse, that every single horse in the stable was valuable. The only difference was that some cost more than others.

He talked about Veronica's attitude problems and her inability to get along with the staff—including his mother—and with the other riders. By the time he was finished, there was almost nothing even Stevie would have added about Veronica's shortcomings, except that she wouldn't have said any of it nearly as nicely as Max had done.

"And now we have to consider what's going on with Danny," Max went on. "The horse ran away yesterday. He's been in the woods almost twenty-four hours and there's no sign of him. There isn't another rider in the stable who wouldn't have set out on a personal search for her horse if he'd run away. Veronica, on the other hand, is right here. Those woods are not a safe place for a horse accustomed to the security of a stable. What do you intend to do about it?" Stevie knew he was glaring straight at Veronica.

"Th-There's the reward . . . ," Veronica stammered.

"We need to talk about that," said her father. An iciness came into his voice as he spoke to his daughter.

"It's been posted," said Max. "Right there on my bulletin board. You can't withdraw it."

"I realize that," said Mr. diAngelo. "What I hadn't realized was Veronica's part in the carelessness that allowed Danny to run away. The reward stands. The only change is that I won't be paying it. Veronica will."

"Daddy!"

"It'll come out of your allowance. Of course, if you find the horse yourself . . ."

"Daddy!"

"It's up to you, Veronica. I think it's time for us to go now."

Aware that the office door was about to open, Stevie gave her friends a hasty shove. By the time the door swung wide, they were in Nickel's stall, crouched down behind the half wall. It took the diAngelos only a few seconds to leave the stable, and that was a good thing, because a few seconds was as long as Stevie could contain her joy at the scene she and her friends had just overheard.

The three of them hugged one another to stifle their giggles and shrieks.

They still wanted to talk with Max but realized that now might not be the very best time. He would still be steaming mad at Veronica, and it was just possible that that anger might extend to anyone in Veronica's age bracket.

"I think we can talk to him later. In the meantime, let's go on a trail ride," Stevie suggested.

They agreed that putting a little distance between themselves and Max was probably a wise idea. They fetched their grooming buckets and tack and headed to their horses' stalls.

Lisa clipped a lead rope on Prancer and brought her out into the hallway to cross-tie her for a quick brush-down. It took just a second to see that something was wrong, and Lisa called Carole and Stevie over to take a look.

Carole ran her hand down the mare's right foreleg and then, for comparison, down the left one. There was no doubt that Prancer had a problem.

"Here, feel this," Carole said, offering Prancer's lower leg to Lisa. Lisa gently took hold of the horse's right leg.

THE SADDLE CLUB

Prancer flinched a bit as she did so. Then Lisa felt the left leg.

"It's warmer and it's swollen," she said.

"Right," Carole said.

"Sure signs of some kind of hurt," Lisa said.

"Probably a strain or something. Usually these things aren't serious and will clear up pretty much on their own, but let's wrap it for now and ask Judy to take a look at it when she comes by. In the meantime, of course, you can't ride Prancer."

Those were words any rider dreaded hearing. It wasn't as if Prancer belonged to Lisa, but she felt as if the mare did. She always rode Prancer. She'd loved Prancer from the first moment she'd set eyes on her. She didn't want to ride any other horse, but this time she didn't have a choice.

"So, now what do I do? Which horse should I ride?" Lisa asked.

Normally Mrs. Reg assigned horses, but she was sick with a cold. When Mrs. Reg wasn't available, Max performed that particular job, but The Saddle Club had already decided they didn't want to talk to Max about *anything*. Red was giving a class, so that left no one free to help them.

"I'm afraid that any schooling horse we choose for you will already be reserved by someone else," Carole said. "I'm not sure what we should do."

"I've got an idea," Stevie said. The mischievous look on her face indicated to her friends that this might be one of her wild schemes.

"And that is?" Carole asked.

"Honey-Pie," said Stevie.

"We're not supposed to ride her," Lisa said.

"Says who?" Stevie countered.

"Paul and Mr. Stookey," said Lisa.

"And what do they know? We all heard Max saying that Honey-Pie should be ridden."

"And we all heard him agree that he'd follow Mr. Stookey's orders, too."

"Maybe we heard that part wrong," Stevie suggested. "There was a lot of noise in the barn then. I'm sure I heard Starlight snorting."

"Isn't that when the big truck was backing in to deliver some grain?" Lisa asked. "That made a lot of noise."

Carole looked at her two friends. She knew what they were up to and she was reluctant to get drawn into trouble with them. On the other hand, the important thing here was what was good for Honey-Pie, and there was no question whatsoever in Carole's mind that Honey-Pie would love a nice trail ride.

It took only a second. "Wasn't Red yelling at a student to keep her heels down?" she asked. "You're right.

There *was* a lot of other noise going on at exactly that moment. We couldn't possibly have heard what Max said, now, could we?"

The pact was sealed. Ten minutes later, the girls were on their way across the field to the woods.

LISA SETTLED INTO the saddle on Honey-Pie's back with total contentment.

"How is she?" Carole asked.

"Every bit as good as we thought she'd be," Lisa said.

"No, I didn't mean how is she to ride, I meant how is she doing?"

"Fine, I think," Lisa said. "She's done everything I've asked of her so far and seems alert and happy. She's stretching her legs, walking smoothly, perking her ears all around and sniffing the air curiously—all signs of a happy horse."

Lisa was amused but not surprised that Carole's question wasn't whether Lisa was enjoying the ride, but whether Honey-Pie was. *Typical Carole!* she thought. In any case, it didn't matter, because both she and the horse were enjoying it.

Honey-Pie didn't have the grace and elegance that Prancer's breeding brought to her gaits, but Honey-Pie's sweet personality came through in her ride. She was completely obedient and obviously making an effort to please.

"I definitely understand why Aunt Emma left all her money to Honey-Pie."

"Sure," Stevie said. "So she wouldn't have to give it all to Paul. Now, let's trot."

It felt good to give way to the pure experience of riding, trotting, enjoying the trail, breathing the fresh air, smelling the wonderful pungent, healthy scent of horse and leather. Lisa put behind her all thoughts of wills and trusts, fiduciary responsibilities, and worthless nephews and surrendered to the moment.

Behind her, Stevie was watching Honey-Pie trot and could sense the horse's pleasure in the simple act of responding to her rider. Unlike Lisa, Stevie wasn't able to focus totally on the moment, however. She was still getting too much pleasure from replaying in her mind the dressing-down that Veronica had received first from Max and then from her father. Stevie wondered how Danny was doing and what he was up to.

Max was right that being alone was a dangerous thing for a pampered horse like Danny, but the fact was that most horses who wandered off usually wandered back when they got hungry and cold. It wasn't likely Danny was lost. It was more likely he was as irritated by Veronica's attitude as everybody else. The problem was that there were dangers in the woods and fields, beyond the reach of human protection. Would Danny be able to look after himself until he decided to return or until someone found him? Or if someone found him, would they perhaps recognize that he was a valuable horse and decide that keeping him was a better idea than returning him?

If that was the case, then the thousand-dollar reward was probably a good idea.

In the lead, Carole brought Starlight down to a walk as the path through the woods narrowed. Honey-Pie slowed down as well, and Belle followed suit. Belle and Starlight had ridden this way often enough to know that this meant they were approaching the creek and they'd have an opportunity for a rest.

Carole turned into the clearing where they always stopped. She halted Starlight and dismounted. Honey-Pie looked around curiously. She sniffed the air. Lisa dismounted and began to lead her to the bush where the girls usually secured their horses, but Honey-Pie, in her own inimitable way, was having none of it. She began nudging Lisa, as she had Carole that first day in the stall when she wanted to go out to the paddock herself. This time it was water she wanted. She gently nudged Lisa all the way to the bank of Willow Creek.

Stevie and Carole laughed as they watched the old mare get the best of their friend. It was fine if Honey-Pie wanted water; what amused them was how she made her wish known.

"One of a kind," said Lisa, holding the reins while Honey-Pie drank her fill of the clear mountain stream.

"One in a million," Stevie corrected her friend.

Once Honey-Pie and her trail mates had had a drink, the girls sat on their favorite rock and simply luxuriated in the chance to do nothing for a few minutes. They didn't feel comfortable being away from the stable for any length of time when they were breaking a rule they all knew they'd heard issued very firmly, but that didn't mean they couldn't take a moment to refresh themselves.

The woods were quiet and peaceful. The only sounds were the usual forest noises. A squirrel rustled in the underbrush. A bird chirped overhead. The creek water burbled past them.

Suddenly there was another sound. It was loud and it

was terrifying. It was the howl of an animal in terrible distress. Belle and Starlight started at the noise, tugging on their reins. The lines were loosely tied to a bush near where the girls sat. Honey-Pie, unaccustomed to the woods, the trail, the creek, and, most especially, the noise, jumped backward. Her ears flattened. Her eyes opened wide so that Lisa could see the whites all around them. The mare stepped back again, tugging at the reins, which slipped right out of the branches where it had been secured.

Before Lisa could even stand up, Honey-Pie, sensing her sudden freedom, fled. She headed straight into the woods, behind a rock, down a hill, and was gone. In a matter of seconds, it seemed, even her hoofbeats were just an echo in Lisa's memory.

SOMETIMES THE SADDLE CLUB could spend hours planning how to solve a problem, devising schemes and backups. Sometimes they acted on instinct. When Honey-Pie fled, there was no planning—it was all instinct.

In a matter of seconds, Carole and Stevie ran to their horses. They knew which direction Honey-Pie had started out in, but they had no idea where she might have turned once she'd rounded the rock and gone down the hill.

"I'll take the left," Carole said. "Stevie, you go that way." She pointed downhill to the right. "And Lisa, you go on foot and follow any signs you can see of Honey-Pie's trail—you know, broken branches, leaves churned up, stuff like that."

"We'd better keep calling to one another," said Lisa. "Otherwise, next thing you know we'll all be lost."

"Bye," said Stevie, not wanting to lose another second.

The path where Honey-Pie had started out wasn't a path at all. It seemed to Lisa that the horse had simply disappeared into the underbrush, and once she began walking into it herself, it was hard to understand how the mare had fit through there at all. The bushes were thick and dense. Honey-Pie must have been powered by a fierce terror to have made it through them so quickly.

Lisa heard the disappearing hoofbeats of her friends' horses and realized that she was now very much alone. She wasn't frightened—not for herself, at least. She wasn't even particularly worried about the trouble she'd be in if something happened to Honey-Pie. What really worried her was the possibility that Honey-Pie could get hurt.

She knew she had to focus if she was going to help the mare. Fretting about what might happen wasn't going to do any good. She had to concentrate on the job at hand.

She grabbed a branch of a bush in front of her and tugged it aside, making a path for herself in the direction where she knew Honey-Pie had gone.

There wasn't a path here. It was pure woods and very overgrown. Lisa and her friends rarely left the wide horse trails in the woods, so this was unfamiliar territory. She knew they were in the foothills of Virginia's mountainous area, but the horse paths were so carefully planned that the riders were rarely aware of any more than a gentle slope. There was nothing gentle about the slope where she found herself now.

Lisa grabbed another branch and held on to it while she let herself down the hillside. Then she was at the big boulder where Honey-Pie had disappeared. The more she thought about it, the more she realized that it had all happened very fast. Honey-Pie had been standing calmly between Belle and Starlight, and then there was that awful sound—what was it?—and then Honey-Pie was racing away. Then she was gone. So very fast.

Lisa could hear Stevie circling to her right and was vaguely aware of Carole, farther away to her left. In her mind, though, she could still hear the awful sound that had frightened Honey-Pie. It had frightened all of them, really, but when it had stopped, nobody had paused to think about what it had been.

Lisa followed her instincts down the hill, thinking that a horse that started running down a hill would keep running down a hill.

"Honey-Pie!" she called out, wondering if the horse would respond to her name. She remembered then the silly image of Ben Stookey standing at the bottom of the ramp on the van, calling Honey-Pie as if she were a dog. Nobody had known at the time just how sweet this horse was. The thought of everything they'd learned about Honey-Pie since then overwhelmed Lisa as she carefully set down one foot, then the next, descending the steep hill. She couldn't stop the tear that rolled down her cheek.

"Honey-Pie!" she cried out, even more loudly this time. There was still no answer.

STEVIE LEANED BACK in Belle's saddle to accommodate the steep downward angle of the path. She stopped every few feet and listened. She knew her eyes were important in this search, but her ears might turn out to be even more important.

"Come on, Belle, do you hear anything?" Stevie listened intently, but she also watched her horse's ears. Belle's hearing was much keener than her own, she knew. Belle was likely to hear the fleeing horse long before Stevie did.

Belle's ears flicked around. When Lisa called Honey-Pie's name, Belle's ears turned toward the sound. Stevie sat up eagerly. Did Lisa's calling mean she had found the horse? She waited for a second, barely breathing. There was no other sound. Lisa was just calling for Honey-Pie. Stevie smiled, recalling how Mr. Stookey had tried to call the horse that way, too. It hadn't worked then, but it had been funny. Now it was nice to have a little something to smile about.

Stevie clucked her tongue against the roof of her mouth and Belle continued downhill, along the path.

It seemed to Stevie that a frightened horse wasn't going to pay much attention to its direction; it was just going to run. And, once running, chances were it would keep heading in pretty much the same direction, dodging trees, rocks, and other natural obstacles, until it could run no farther. Stevie had no idea what obstacles Honey-Pie might have encountered, but she did know the general direction the horse had started out in, and it made sense to her to keep going that way.

She stopped again and looked around. This time there were no sounds. Belle's ears stood straight up. Nothing.

They went on.

"OUCH!" LISA SAID involuntarily. She'd scraped her hand on a rock as she grabbed for a branch. "Why couldn't you have run away in a field?" she said, now a little annoyed at the daunting task of searching the woods for a horse that seemed to have disappeared from the face of the earth.

And there was no sign of the horse. Nothing. There were no noises, no rustling, no whinnies. Perhaps Honey-Pie *had* disappeared, been picked up by aliens in a ship. *No, no.* Lisa shook her head. She was beginning to think like Stevie.

The ground leveled then, making Lisa's progress easier, but progress to where? She had no idea whether she was anywhere near the horse.

She stopped and looked around to see if she could tell where she was. She hadn't gone far and shouldn't have trouble finding her way back to the clearing by the creek. What she didn't know was whether she would have any success in looking for Honey-Pie.

Overhead, a squirrel dashed along a branch, making an eager clucking sound. Was he trying to tell her something? Probably not. Squirrels were not noted for their intelligence.

Lisa took a few steps, then paused to catch her breath. There was something horsey, familiar. What was it? She took in another lungful of fresh Virginia air. There was definitely something horsey about it. It had the distinct odor of manure.

She looked at the ground. There, not far from her,

were two balls of manure. Lisa didn't think it would have been possible for her to be happy at the sight of manure, but she definitely was. Where there was manure, there was a horse, and these were decidedly fresh droppings. She *was* on the right trail. Now all she had to do was find the next bit of manure!

She sniffed again; she scanned the ground. The two balls lay a few inches apart. The next one had to be straight ahead. She began to follow an imaginary line and crossed her fingers.

CAROLE LEANED FORWARD, ducking under a branch that hung low over the horse trail. She had decided it made sense to follow the widest trail that kept to the contour of the hill, suspecting that if Honey-Pie had happened upon this trail her protective instincts would have kept her on it. The trail looped around, coming back to Pine Hollow. It would be the best news in the world if she found the horse somewhere along this comfortable, safe path. Carole knew wishful thinking when she was dealing with it, but there was some logic involved as well.

She paused every few steps, listening and looking, as she knew her friends were doing. The trail divided ahead. Carole had forgotten that fork. One part of the path continued uphill and the other went down, paralleling the creek all the way to the field. They didn't take this lower trail very often because it skirted one of the rare ravines in these woods. It was rocky and could be dangerous. Max often warned young riders away from it.

What convinced Carole to follow it was not that she was certain she'd find Honey-Pie there, but that she knew it was the part of the woods where Honey-Pie would be most likely to get in trouble—the only place where she might really need their help to get out.

A sudden realization swept over her and she felt a surge of cold perspiration. *The gorge. The gorge. Anything but that!*

THERE IT WAS, another ball of manure. Lisa knew she was going in the right direction, and part of her was very happy about that. Another part wasn't happy at all. She was getting closer and closer to the bed of Willow Creek, and just across the creek, on the side of the hill that seemed so gentle right where she stood, was an area that wasn't gentle at all. What if . . . ?

She stifled the thought and pressed forward.

"Honey-Pie!" she cried out. "Honey-Pie!" Still no answer.

The land rose to the left and Lisa followed it, knowing exactly where it would lead her. Her breath came in small gulps and her heart began pounding.

She wasn't at all surprised to see Carole following the path that came from above her on the hillside. She knew that Carole knew, too.

"Where's Stevie?" Carole asked.

"Not far," Lisa said. "I heard her—"

"You guys?" Stevie said, the worry apparent in her voice. "You know what I think?"

"Yeah, we know," Lisa said. "We've all figured it out."

They all stopped. There were still no sounds, no horse in distress, no whinnying, nickering, chomping, stamping.

Belle's ears perked forward.

"Let's go see," said Stevie.

It wasn't far to the edge. They almost didn't want to get there, but they knew they had to.

Where the land had broken away to form the ravine, they saw the first definite signs of the bad news they feared but somehow expected. A scramble of hoofprints told the story of a desperate but failed effort to stay on top of the hillside.

"Honey-Pie!" Lisa called before looking over the edge. She didn't want to look, and neither did her friends.

There was a snort and a whinny in response. They'd found her.

Lisa neared the edge of the steep hillside, and, holding on to a secure tree branch, she looked over.

"She's there!" Lisa said. "She's standing and she's okay, but she's not alone!"

"Danny!" Carole said breathlessly.

"Wow! A thousand bucks!" said Stevie.

13

IT SEEMED LIKE good news, and of course it was, but the girls knew their work wasn't done. Stevie and Carole dismounted, secured their horses—firmly—to tree branches, and joined Lisa at the edge of the ravine.

Knowing the horses were there was not the same thing as knowing they were okay, and it was far from the same thing as rescuing them.

"A helicopter!" Stevie said. "I mean, between the two of them, those horses are richer than almost anybody in Willow Creek. Honey-Pie could hire a helicopter to get the two of them out of there!"

"Well, that just leaves the little matter of letting everybody know how many rules we broke," said Lisa.

"I think they're going to know anyway," Carole said.

"They'll know about some, sure, but maybe they don't have to know absolutely everything."

"Maybe," Carole said. "Look, let's go see what the situation is down there."

"Easier said than done," Lisa remarked, looking at the steep climb ahead of them.

"We have to crisscross it," Stevie said. "We can't go straight down or we'll fall. If we go first to the left there and then switch back to the right, I think it'll work."

Carole looked where Stevie pointed.

"It might at that," Carole agreed. She stood up and began the treacherous climb down to the horses.

The girls zigzagged slowly down the hill. Carole was the first to reach the horses. Honey-Pie nuzzled her affectionately. Danny backed off. That was the difference between the two horses: One was nervous and frightened, while the other was completely calm. Carole patted Honey-Pie and checked her for injuries.

The mare didn't move an inch. She was utterly obedient.

The dirt on Honey-Pie's flank told the tale of her descent into the valley. Undignified, perhaps, but totally successful. Carole checked her legs carefully; everything was fine. There was no swelling, there were no warm spots, and the mare didn't flinch at all.

"She's completely fit," Carole said. "At least as far as I can tell."

Danny was still shying from his rescuers. Carole knew he was a well-behaved horse and would do what he was asked if he was asked in the right way. She unclipped the lead rope that was still attached to Honey-Pie's bridle and handed it to Stevie to attach to Danny's halter. A slight tug brought him to a stop. Lisa checked him over while Stevie convinced him to remain still.

"Danny wasn't so lucky," Lisa said. "Look, here's some swelling in his hind leg, and he's got scratches on his chest."

Carole checked the leg and agreed with Lisa. Danny was definitely uncomfortable. Stevie tugged at the lead rope again and walked him a few yards from where he'd been standing so that Carole could see how much he favored the sore leg.

"He can put weight on it," Carole said, very relieved. At least he could walk and wouldn't have to be treated right there.

Stevie pulled her sweatshirt up over her head and fashioned a makeshift leg wrap.

"It might help, it might not," she said.

"It can't hurt," Carole remarked.

"Okay, now, how do we get them out of here?"

116

She and her friends looked up at the hill. It seemed an even steeper climb going up than it had going down, but it was the only way out. On the other side, there was a wall of rock that was out of the question.

"One horse at a time," Lisa said.

"Danny first since he's the one who's hurt," said Stevie. That made sense. She tugged at the lead rope to make him walk toward the beginning of the path the girls had chosen.

He didn't budge.

Stevie tugged again, gently. No good. She tugged hard. Nothing.

"I think he's freaked," said Lisa. "He must have had a really bad fall."

The girls looked at one another. They knew they had a couple of options. They could make a blindfold. Sometimes if a horse didn't know where he was going, he went more willingly.

They only needed to figure out which piece of clothing would make the best blindfold.

They chose Lisa's windbreaker. She was taking it off and rolling it to fit Danny's face when a curious thing happened.

Honey-Pie intruded. She walked over to Danny and began licking him. It was something the girls

117

had seen many times before, but never with two adult horses. Honey-Pie was licking Danny just as if he were her newborn foal. She was mothering him. She managed to get some of the mud off him. The girls stood stone still, awed by what they were seeing.

Honey-Pie continued washing the wounded, full-grown gelding the same way she must have tended to her own helpless babies at the moment of birth. Danny, once frozen in terror, relaxed at the soothing rub of a mother's tongue. Honey-Pie paused and looked at her handiwork. Besides getting some of the mud off, she'd also licked his scrapes clean. She must have thought it was good enough for now, because she nudged him.

It was a familiar motion. It was the same nudge she'd given Carole that first day in the barn, and it was how she'd pushed Lisa aside to get a drink of water earlier that day. This horse knew what she wanted and she knew how to get it.

Danny looked at her, mild irritation evident in his stare. Honey-Pie paid him no mind. She nudged again. Danny stepped forward. Another nudge. Danny moved again, this time toward the path.

Stevie tugged at the lead line. Danny stopped dead and glared at her. He wasn't going to listen to Stevie at all, but he *was* going to do what Honey-Pie told him, even if he didn't want to.

Nudge, step, nudge, step.

None of the girls said anything. They were afraid to break the spell.

Step by step, Honey-Pie moved Danny to the hillside. Carole began walking ahead to show Honey-Pie the way. Honey-Pie figured it out. Nudge, step, nudge, step.

It took a long time and felt like an eternity, but the progress never stopped. Honey-Pie never relented as she ordered her foster foal up the hillside, step by step.

And then they were at the top.

Stevie, still holding Danny's lead rope, found that all his resistance had gone. Although his leg was bothering him, he seemed willing to be told what to do.

What Stevie and her friends wanted him to do was to get back to Pine Hollow.

"It might be a good idea to take a little rest," Carole said. Both horses had just made a very difficult climb under the most unusual circumstances and had to be tired.

"It might be a better idea to go back to where Danny can get some medical care and we can get . . ." Lisa paused.

"Yelled at?" Stevie supplied.

"Well, that, too," said Lisa.

For the first time in a few hours, the girls had something to smile about. They were ready to go home.

"Look, I think good old Honey-Pie's had enough exercise for the day," Lisa said. "I'll walk and lead her. You two ride, and Stevie, you keep Danny on the lead rope, okay?"

"Deal," Stevie agreed.

Lisa took Honey-Pie's reins and tugged in the direction of the trail that would lead them home. Honey-Pie, however, refused to budge.

"What's going on with you?" Lisa asked, tugging again. "Are you okay?"

Honey-Pie's response was to nudge Lisa—toward her own saddle. Lisa shook her head and tugged. Honey-Pie stood her ground and nudged.

"I think she wants you to get in the saddle," Stevie translated.

"I think I understood that," Lisa said. "I just don't *understand* it."

"It's simple," Stevie said. "Remember how my dad told us what a great broodmare and mother this horse is—uh, was . . . uh, whatever?"

"Yeah," Lisa said.

"She's like almost any mother I've ever known, then.

120

She wants to be the boss of the whole wide world and she's not going to be happy until you do exactly what she tells you to do."

Lisa sighed. She was used to dealing with strong-willed mothers. She just wasn't used to having the mother be a horse.

"All right, then," she said to the mare, reaching for the left stirrup with her toe. "I'll do this now, but I absolutely refuse to go to the mall with you after dinner!"

Honey-Pie seemed satisfied with the deal. As soon as Lisa was settled in the saddle, the three riders and four horses went where they most wanted to go: home.

14

WHAT WAS WAITING for them at Pine Hollow was trouble, and it was standing in a row at the edge of the schooling ring. Max was there and Mrs. Reg, as well as Max's wife, Deborah. Veronica was there, too, along with her parents, and so were Paul and Mr. Stookey.

Max had a pair of field glasses. He was the first one to spot them. As soon as he did, the ranks broke and everybody who had been waiting ran to greet them—some happy to see them, some not so happy.

The first words out of Veronica's mouth were, "What have you done to Danny?"

The question almost took Stevie's breath away because it was so utterly *Veronica*. "Rescued him," she said, but she didn't offer any details.

Veronica eyed the homemade bandage with disdain. "Just a little swelling," Carole said. "He'll be fine."

"But the scratches!"

There was no way to satisfy Veronica, ever. None of the girls thought it was worth trying.

"Is she okay?" Ben Stookey asked, looking at the now obviously tired Honey-Pie.

"She's just wonderful," Lisa said. "This is one of the world's greatest horses. As far as we're concerned, she's worth every penny of her bank account—and then some. You just wouldn't believe—"

Carole coughed, shushing Lisa. Lisa looked at her quizzically but kept quiet. They could talk later.

"She's really okay?" That was Paul speaking. His words might have been intended to convey concern, but the tone of his voice betrayed pure disappointment.

"Really okay," Stevie confirmed. "Just ready for a rest."

Paul's lips tightened into a thin, straight line. He had nothing more to say.

Then Max reached them. He did have something to say. "I think it would be a good idea if we had a little talk in my office," he said in a very controlled voice. "After you've looked after your—and Mr. Stookey's—horses." He turned to Veronica. "You can take care of Danny now, can't you?" he asked. Veronica nodded and took the lead line from Stevie without a word or a sign of thanks.

The girls took as long as they could to groom, water, and feed their horses. They were not looking forward to their meeting with Max.

"I DON'T GET you three," Max began much more calmly than they had thought he might. "Do you have any idea how important it is to Pine Hollow to have a horse like Honey-Pie stabled here? The three of you are perfectly willing to risk my reputation by flouting my specific instructions, and my promise to a misguided owner, by taking that horse out on a trail ride—which was exactly what she needed, every bit as much as she needed to be longed—and to chance annoying the ignorant owners by caring for their horse the way she ought to be cared for?"

The girls exchanged glances. They were hearing this wrong.

"What took you so long?" Max demanded.

"You mean to get back?"

"No!" he bellowed. "To take her out on the trail. The three of you are willing to ignore all kinds of sensible rules and regulations. How come it took you so long to break the silliest order any owner ever gave me about a horse?"

"I don't get it," Carole whispered.

"You don't have to," Stevie whispered back. "Max isn't angry at us."

"I am a little," said Max. "You should have let me know that Paul was giving you orders."

"We weren't paying any attention to his orders," said Lisa. "Only we didn't know why he was doing it until last night."

"You might have told us what was going on with all that fiduciary and trustee stuff. We could have understood it. You could have trusted us," Stevie said.

"Maybe," Max said. "Well, look. You did break an order and you did it in a way that let absolutely everybody here know you did it."

"Yes, we know," Lisa said.

"My mother tells me there's a lot of tack that needs a lot of attention," said Max.

"We've got to clean it all?" Stevie asked.

"Until you can see the reflection of your faces in the gleaming leather!" Max said.

"Yes sir!" Carole said, standing up.

Stevie stood up, too, and gave Lisa a hand to help her to her feet. She thought it would be a good idea to get out of Max's office before he got any more ideas relating to things like manure piles.

* * *

"WE'RE THE LUCKIEST GIRLS in the world," Lisa said an hour later as she finished making her third saddle gleam.

"Because we get to ride a lot?" Carole asked.

"No, because we've just had a very fine day and we've spent almost all of it with horses," Stevie said.

"Okay, so let's see if we can list all the fine things that happened," Lisa suggested.

"We saved two horses' lives," said Carole.

"Maybe not," Stevie corrected her. "I'm not sure we had much to do with saving Danny. I think all the work was done by Honey-Pie."

"Hey, why wouldn't you let me tell Mr. Stookey about that?" Lisa asked Carole, recalling the cough that had cut her tale short.

"Oh, easy," said Stevie. "See, if we have to tell them about the wonderful job Honey-Pie did, we have to let them know she did it because she ran off—and incidentally, my theory is that awful noise was actually Danny crying out when he fell—"

"Me too," Carole said, having come to the same conclusion.

"Me three," Lisa added.

"And if they don't know she ran off, they don't know that we didn't tie her securely enough—"

"That horse can be so stubborn, nothing would have held her when she decided to go to Danny," Lisa said, remembering the nudging Honey-Pie had given her.

"Well, let me just say that there are a few things people don't actually have to know about what happened today, and all of them have to do with us looking careless," said Stevie.

"Okay," Lisa agreed.

"Now, the next question—"

Veronica came into the tack room and seemed displeased to find them there. "Oh, you're here," she said.

"For a while," Stevie said, indicating the dwindling pile of tack lined up for a careful cleaning.

"Daddy asked me to find out who I should make out the check to," she said.

It had been a while since any of them had thought about the reward. A thousand dollars.

"Can we get back to you in a minute?" Carole asked. "We need to talk."

"If you're going to argue about it, I'm not sure I'll give it to any of you," she said, then turned on her heel and left the tack room.

"She doesn't get it, does she?" Lisa asked, shaking her head.

"No, and she never will, so don't bother trying to teach her," Stevie said.

"Okay, so what do we do?" Carole said.

"There's no question who really found and rescued Danny," Lisa said. "Honey-Pie."

"My thought exactly," Carole said. "There are two things wrong with that. The first is that we've just agreed nobody ever really needs to know all the details of that."

"And the second is, what is a horse going to do with a thousand dollars?" said Lisa.

"Especially a horse that already has two million!"

"But the problem is that we don't really deserve that money," Carole said earnestly.

"Well, should we just say 'No, thank you'?" Lisa suggested.

"And take away the joy of knowing that it's coming out of Veronica's allowance?" Stevie responded, horrified.

"No, no, don't worry. We'll never do that," Lisa assured her.

"So, who gets the money?"

"Sports cars, expensive clothes, alligator wallets, yachts . . . ," Stevie said dreamily.

"It's not that much money," Lisa said.

"But it's enough," Carole said.

"For what?" Stevie asked.

"For a nice—a really nice—secondhand horse trailer."

Lisa and Stevie smiled, understanding Carole's perfect solution.

Carole rose and left her friends for a few minutes. She found Veronica in the stable office, picking up a piece of paper from Mrs. Reg's desk.

"You can make the check out to CARL," Carole said, interrupting Veronica's snooping.

"Carole, you mean?" Veronica asked.

"No, CARL," Carole told her. "The County Animal Rescue League. Tell your dad it'll be tax-deductible," she added. "That'll make him happy."

Veronica didn't speak. She just dropped the paper she was holding back on the desk and left. Carole stood still, savoring the moment.

Before she returned to her friends, her curiosity overwhelmed her and she glanced at the paper that had been so interesting to Veronica. She had to look at it twice, and the second look confirmed what the first one had told her. She rushed back.

"You won't believe it!" she said.

"She gave you cash?" Stevie said.

"No, not that, but it was wonderful. It's absolutely perfect to make her pay for something to take 'old nags' around town to get the veterinary care she doesn't think they deserve. We are *wonderful!*"

"So what aren't we going to believe?" Stevie asked.

"This was a better day than we even knew," Carole said smugly.

"So?" Lisa urged.

"Well, Veronica was snooping when I found her and I sort of couldn't resist, although you know I really don't like snooping and think that what's on people's desks is their business and not mine and I wouldn't like it if someone—"

"Carole!" Stevie said in frustration.

"It was a legal thingy," Carole said. "At the top it said a whole bunch of stuff about the authority of the Cross County district attorney, blah, blah, blah—"

"Carole!" Lisa said.

"It's a restraining order. It says that Paul Fredericks isn't allowed within a hundred yards of Honey-Pie!"

"That's to protect her from him!" Lisa said gleefully.

"So he can't find a way to kill her and get his hands on Honey-Pie's bank account!" Stevie said.

"Perfect," Lisa agreed.

"Aunt Emma's fortune will stay in Honey-Pie's worthy and deserving . . . uh, hmmm . . . hooves," Stevie said.

"I don't think I've ever had a more satisfying day,"

said Carole. "I mean, if you forget the part about searching fruitlessly, risking our lives going down that hill, letting Honey-Pie put herself in danger, getting Max angry at us—you know, all that stuff."

"My favorite part is sticking it to Veronica," Stevie said. "That makes any day perfect."

"Well, there is one thing that's pretty bad," said Lisa.

Her friends looked at her.

"I think we've lost our opportunity to have a sail on Paul's yacht."

The girls laughed. It seemed a very small price to pay for such a victory.

ABOUT THE AUTHOR

BONNIE BRYANT is the author of more than a hundred books about horses, including The Saddle Club series, The Saddle Club Super Editions, the Pony Tails series, and Pine Hollow, which follows the Saddle Club girls into their teens. She has also written novels and movie novelizations under her married name, B. B. Hiller.

Ms. Bryant began writing The Saddle Club in 1986. Although she had done some riding before that, she intensified her studies then and found herself learning right along with her characters Stevie, Carole, and Lisa. She claims that they are all much better riders than she is.

Ms. Bryant was born and raised in New York City. She still lives there, in Greenwich Village, with her two sons.